A Clear Spring

A Clear Spring
by Barbara Wilson

Red Sand, Blue Sky
by Cathy Applegate

A Clear Spring

Barbara Wilson

Girl's First!

The Feminist Press
at the City University of New York

Published by the Feminist Press at the City University of New York
The Graduate Center, 365 Fifth Avenue
New York, New York 10016
feministpress.org

First Feminist Press edition, 2002

Library of Congress Cataloging-in-Publication Data

Wilson, Barbara, 1950–
A clear spring / Barbara Wilson.
p. cm. — (Girls first! ; 1)
Summary: While visiting relatives in Seattle, tweleve-year-old Willa explores the ethnic diversity of her family and investigates the pollution of a salmon stream.
ISBN 1-55861-277-7 (pbk. : alk. paper)
[1. Pollution—Fiction. 2. Environmental protection—Fiction. 3. Seattle (Wash.)—Fiction. 4. Panamanian Americans—Fiction. 5. Racially mixed people—Fiction.] I. Title. II. Series.

PZ7.W6896 C1 2002
[Fic]—dc21 2001033970

The Feminist Press would like to thank Mariam K. Chamberlain, Florence Howe, Joanne Markell, Genevieve Vaughan, Henny Wenkart, and Patricia Wentworth and Mark Fagan for their generosity in supporting this book.

Cover illustration © 2002 by Karen Ritz
Text design and composition by Dayna Navaro
Printed in Canada on acid-free paper by Transcontinental Printning
06 05 04 03 02 5 4 3 2 1

To our nieces Aja and Azizi Dotson,
Eleanor Roach, and Michelle Wilson

Chapter 1

The summer Willa C. Lopez flew out to Seattle to visit her aunts, she was twelve, even though most people still said she was eleven. Technically she *was* eleven, because her birthday was in mid-August, and it was only the twentieth of June.

Technically, Willa thought in disgust. Adults were so needlessly hairsplitting. "This is my eleven-year-old daughter," her mother had said to the airline agent in Chicago.

But Willa wrote it down differently in the fresh new journal she was keeping of this trip. "At twelve years old, I am making my first trip to Seattle," she wrote, leaning her arm carefully on the pull-down tray so that her neighbor, a sleepy businessman with the *New York Times* in front of his face, couldn't catch a glimpse.

Again, that wasn't technically true. She'd been to Seattle once as a baby, when her parents were still married. But she didn't remember it, so it didn't really count. Only things you remember count, Willa believed.

Willa didn't like to remember everything, just as she didn't like to be too technical about facts. Facts were boring. Facts were on tests. Facts were sometimes hard. Facts could even hurt.

She stared out the window at the endless fields below. They were mostly huge green circles inside brown squares. At the center must be a watering system that swung out in wide circles to irrigate the crops. There were a lot of these, a huge quilt of them stitched over the Midwest.

Willa had expected to be more excited about flying across the country by herself, and at the start she was. She'd rearranged her belongings around her many times. That's what the flight attendant had called them, "personal belongings," which made them seem more than just books and a water bottle and her new journal.

She'd gotten the journal from her friend Emma just before she left. She and Emma had been best friends since fourth grade. But now, just thinking about Emma made Willa's throat get tight.

Emma had a new best friend whose name was Parker. Parker was everything Willa was not: athletic, popular, smart. She even wrote poetry—good poetry. She had swooped down on Emma last year, around Christmastime, and had taken her away. Even though Emma had said, "We can all be friends," it hadn't really worked out that way. Willa and Emma weren't best friends anymore. That was a fact, and it hurt.

There was a movie on the flight, but it involved a bunch of stupid car chases. She'd read through her favorite book already and the other one no longer looked interesting. Memories of saying good-bye to her mother at the airport began to bubble up, the way water comes up from the kitchen drain when something's stuck in the pipe.

Ed, her older brother, hadn't been with them at O'Hare Airport. He was already at Papa's in San Diego, where he'd spend his summer swimming and playing softball. Usually Willa went to Papa's for a few weeks every summer, too, but this year his wife, Cindi, had a new baby, and everybody seemed to think it might be too much to have Willa for a visit. It was different with Ed, they said. He was sixteen and could drive now. He didn't need to be supervised.

"I don't need to be supervised," Willa had said.

Her mother had just rolled her eyes.

Willa had once read a newsletter in which her mother was described as a "high-powered executive." Maybe Laura Saunders was high-powered at American Gypsum, but at home she was often just tired. She was known for shaking her head no, as she did when Willa had proposed that she just stay home in the apartment that summer.

"No. I'll send you to summer camp again with Emma, and then you can go to a day camp in the city. You'll be with your friends. You and Emma and that girl Parker, who seems so nice."

Willa opened her journal and wrote, "That would have completely WRECKED the summer. Having to be in camp DAY AND NIGHT with Emma and Parker. My mom and I had a big fight about it. She kept saying, 'But I thought you liked going to camp with Emma.' She doesn't understand anything."

But then her mom had gotten a phone call from Aunt Ceci in Seattle.

Willa could hear her mom on the phone, saying things like: "Seattle seems so far away." "Don't you and Janie have to work?" "Oh, I see." "Yes, there's Carmen, too."

Willa had heard her mother's voice sink a little when she said *Carmen,* but it bounced up again as Laura Saunders considered. "Well, if you get off at three, and Janie is able to work at home or take Willa with her . . . and of course Willa can be on her own for a few hours here and there. She's very responsible, really."

Willa wrote in her journal, "My Aunt Ceci is a carpenter, and Janie is some kind of nature teacher. My Aunt Carmen used to be a singer in a band, and now she's an actress and is married and has two girls about my age, Phyllis and Tabby. Ceci and Carmen are my dad's sisters."

They'd talked about Carmen at the airport. "Your Aunt Carmen is a very sweet woman, but she's also a little apt to fly off the handle. Carmen and your dad don't quite see eye to eye. But I guess you know that already."

Willa wasn't sure what the trouble was between her father and Aunt Carmen. Once she'd asked what happened, and her mother had said, "It's just that they're both proud people. Too proud to admit they're wrong."

Willa had wondered if that was part of the problem with her mother and father, too.

Willa noticed she'd written in her journal, "I really miss my mom. I miss Emma."

She hadn't meant to write that. She'd meant to write, "I'm so excited to be going by myself to Seattle!"

Chapter 2

Aunt Ceci had assured her that the flight into Seattle would be awesome. "Keep your eyes peeled for Mount Rainier. There's a whole chain of volcanic mountains along the northwest coast, and Mount Rainier is the biggest."

Willa kept her eyes peeled, but she didn't see anything except thick white and gray clouds. The businessman next to her woke up from a nap and said gloomily, "It's *always* like this in early summer in the Northwest. If you're not wearing sweaters at the Fourth of July picnic, you're wearing raincoats." He was originally from Texas and had been moved out to Seattle by his company. He the missed the barbecue and even the tornados.

Willa thought worriedly about the pile of T-shirts

and shorts in her suitcase. Then bigger doubts began to spread, getting as big as the soft clouds the plane was descending through.

She was about to spend two whole months with people she didn't know very well. For two months she'd be away from her mother, from Chicago, from everything that was familiar. Why was her mother sending her away? Why didn't Papa want to have her stay? Why did they have to get divorced?

Even though it had been a long time ago that the divorce happened—six years—and even though Papa was married again and had a new baby, Willa still sometimes wished her parents would get back together.

She used to talk about that with her brother, Ed. When he was younger, he'd agreed that when people got married, they should *stay* married. But now he was older and wiser. He'd had a girlfriend and had broken up with her after two months to be with another girl, and now he was broken up with *her* too. It didn't seem to bother him, and he said things like, "Not everybody is meant to be together forever, kid."

As the plane taxied to a stop, she wished suddenly, fiercely, that instead of Seattle, she had landed in San Diego. She wanted Ed to be waiting for her, and Papa. And even Cindi.

"Willa!" called Aunt Ceci, and as Willa came through the gate she was wrapped close in a big hug. She relaxed. Aunt Ceci was here, and she was completely familiar from her photographs. Besides, she looked a lot like Papa, the same curly black hair, bright dark eyes, and high cheekbones. Aunt Ceci was wearing a brown fleece vest that was as soft as fur. It was like being hugged by a nice warm cat.

But where was Janie? Surrounding Aunt Ceci was a crowd of tall African Americans who also seemed vaguely familiar. In their midst was a lighter-skinned woman in a red suit, with red lipstick and a big sweep of black hair, who also looked a lot like her father.

"Willa," she said. "Baby!"

It was Aunt Carmen and her family: James North, her husband, and her daughters, Phyllis and Tabitha. But everyone was so big. Carmen never sent photographs, and everyone had grown up.

The younger girl, Tabby, was tall and skinny, with wiry long hair and small round glasses that sat playfully on her solemn face. Phyllis was not only tall, but strong and bulky, with a lot of muscle in her arms and legs. She was serious looking, too. She didn't smile, but looked Willa over carefully.

"Phyllis will be a junior this fall, but you and Tabby are the same age, I think. Aren't you eleven?"

"Mama," said Tabby quickly, speaking for the first time, "I'm still ten until my birthday, September eighth."

"I'm twelve," said Willa decisively. Tabby was going into the sixth grade, and Willa would be in the seventh. There was a *huge* difference between elementary and junior high school.

The adults began shouting out their ages—thirty-six, thirty-nine, forty-three—as if it was all a big joke.

Tabby and Willa looked at each other and sighed. Tabby had a dimple in one cheek, Willa noticed. When she gave a little smile, like now, it showed.

Suddenly a woman with short, spiky burgundy hair, wearing baggy yellow pants and a green T-shirt that said "Save the Salmon" ran up. Her eyes were green and fringed with black lashes. She seemed to know everybody, including Willa.

"Willa!" she gave Willa a big hug. "Sorry I'm late. I had to park. How was the flight?" She was bubbling with excitement.

It must be Janie. But in the photographs, Janie had blond hair and glasses. Willa knew that Janie and Ceci had lived together for ten years, but this was first time Willa had met her, and Willa felt a little shy.

Janie looked too young and too wild to be her aunt's partner. But Janie's smile was so contagious that Willa couldn't help relaxing and hugging her back. She let herself be led away to the baggage claim to find the suitcase she'd carefully packed last night.

Chapter 3

Tabby wanted to be a chef. She said so in the pizzeria where they all went on the way home.

"She's been helping us cook since she was about six," said Aunt Carmen proudly. "Now she makes practically all the family meals."

"Somebody has to," said Phyllis, "with Dad working late, and you at rehearsals, and me at basketball practice."

"If I didn't cook," said Tabby, "we'd just eat junk food. But Janie and I made an organic vegetable garden in our yard. You just open the back door and there all the food is!"

Willa was astounded. She didn't know anyone in Chicago who had a vegetable garden, much less an organic one. Emma and Willa's other friends lived in apartment buildings like hers. She could remember a time a long ago, when she was little and lived in San Diego, they'd had a backyard with palms and an avocado and an orange tree. You could pick an orange right off the tree. You could pick an avocado, too, but they were so strangely green and soft that she didn't bother. In Chicago all she ever saw were regular old trees on the street, flowers in spring and summer, and houseplants in windows.

"Have you thought about what you want to be, Willa?" Aunt Ceci asked. She was a comforting presence next to Willa, with her smile so much like Papa's.

Willa thought about it, but nothing came to her, except that she didn't really want to work in a big office building in downtown Chicago. She shook her head.

"I don't know either," said Phyllis. "If I could, I'd be a basketball star, but probably in the long run I'd rather be a photographer."

"I studied English literature in college," said Aunt Ceci, "but when I graduated, I knew I wanted to work outside and make something with my hands."

"I knew I wanted the outdoors life, too," said Uncle James. "I was out in the field for Seattle City Light a long time, shimmying up and down those telephone poles. But now I've got it easy. I just drive around in my little car and inspect people's home wiring. I got a little old for the heights," he smiled. Uncle James had some gray hair now, but Willa thought she could still see in him a tall, skinny boy who liked to climb trees.

"That makes three of us outdoors people," said Janie. "I loved bugs when I was a kid. It never occurred to me that you could make any kind of living from being a bug-lover, though. My parents had a farm in Oregon, so they were mostly interested in killing bugs!"

"I always wanted to sing and act," said Aunt Carmen. "Right from the beginning, I knew."

"It's true," said Aunt Ceci with a laugh. "Carmen was always getting me and Tommy to appear in her shows. She'd be the star and we'd be the clowns or something. The neighbor kids all had to pay a nickel to see her."

"You'll have to come and see me in my play this summer, Willa," said Aunt Carmen. "I'm a very grand lady in it."

They were suddenly all talking at once about other plays and musicals. Aunt Carmen had been in *Cabaret*, *Cat on a Hot Tin Roof,* and some Shakespeare plays.

Uncle James said, "The best was when your aunt was in a musical called *Dogs,* kind of a takeoff on *Cats.* She used to rehearse by barking when the doorbell rang. Until the day the minister's wife came for a visit."

"That man can tell a tale," said Aunt Carmen as everybody laughed. "In fact, I was an Irish Setter with several very important songs."

Willa had seen *Cats* in Chicago. Her mother had taken her lots of times to plays, she told them.

"Willa's mom, Laura, was the star of our Shakespeare class in college," Aunt Ceci told them all. "She was in my American literature class, too. When she named you Willa, I wasn't surprised. Willa Cather was her favorite author. How your mother loved books—no wonder she became a librarian."

"I didn't know she was a librarian," said Janie. "I thought she was somebody big at American Gypsum."

"My mom used to be a librarian," said Willa. "Then she had to get a job that paid more."

Aunt Carmen said softly, "That Tomás, you never could count on him."

"It's late," said Uncle James firmly. "And it's even later for Willa. She's still on Chicago time."

They said good-bye to Aunt Carmen and her family and drove to Ceci and Janie's house. It was white and old and little shabby, but there was a welcoming light in the windows, and flowers grew in every corner of the front yard. The only flowers Willa recognized were the roses. Inside, the front room was painted different shades of gold and green, and the soft green rug was like moss.

Aunt Ceci led her up a steep flight of stairs. There were three doors on the narrow landing. The one in the middle was painted lipstick red, and the other two were warm yellow.

"This will be your room," said Aunt Ceci, opening one of the yellow doors and leading Willa into a small room with a curved ceiling and single large window. There was a bed, a desk, and a chest of drawers, all painted yellow.

Aunt Ceci left Willa to get ready for bed. When she returned she had an extra blanket.

"It probably seems a lot cooler to you here than Chicago."

"Yes," admitted Willa. "I've never seen anybody wearing a fleece vest in summer in Chicago!"

Aunt Ceci laughed. "Maybe you want to wear it yourself."

"Sure!" The brown fleece vest was warm and

smelled of Aunt Ceci—lavender and sawdust. Just putting it on made Willa feel cozy, as if her old Pooh Bear was snuggling close to her.

"Would you like me to keep you company a while?" Aunt Ceci asked.

"Okay. . . ," said Willa. She wanted to ask why Aunt Carmen had said that thing about not being able to count on Papa, but she was shy. Instead she said, "Would you tell me about Grandma and Grandpa and Panama?" But even as Aunt Ceci started to describe the place her family came from, Willa's eyelids closed. She fell asleep imagining she was in a Central American rainforest, lying in the arms of a nice brown bear.

Chapter 4

Willa woke to sunshine and the sound of sparrows outside the window. It was very early, but when she went downstairs wearing her pajamas and brown vest, Aunt Ceci had already left for work.

Willa found a note: "Good morning, Willa! Help yourself to cereal, fruit, toast. Make yourself at home. Janie, the lazy bum, always sleeps in till seven-thirty. I'll see you later!"

Quietly, Willa poured herself a bowl of granola and milk, then took it up the stairs. They were so steep and narrow that they were like something in a ship. On the landing the lipstick red door beckoned with possibility. When she opened it, cautiously, she found a long, narrow room with a low sloped ceiling. Cardboard boxes were piled in stacks with labels like "photographs" on them. There were no windows and it was stuffy with an old-fashioned smell. Not a place you'd want to hang out in very long, but a good hiding place if you needed one sometime. Willa backed out and turned to the yellow door across the landing from her bedroom.

She remembered Aunt Ceci saying last night that it was Janie's office, but it was like no office Willa had ever seen. It wasn't like her father's real estate office in San Diego, which always had a frantic feeling. It wasn't at all like her mother's office at American Gypsum, which was always spotless. Next to Mom's computer were a few piles of paper and by the phone was a notepad, but otherwise it was so neat that it was hard to figure out what her mother did there.

Janie's office looked like a playroom. True, there was a laptop computer, but it was half buried in newspapers and magazines, scraps of paper and leaflets, on a huge table that also held a bird's nest, twigs and leaves, some bottles of water, and a microscope. From the ceiling hung a dried bat, and a box in the corner was filled with tiny bird bones. Small plastic containers were piled all around, labeled with handwritten notes: "Soil samples, April," read one. "Bark," read another. "Scat—various animals," read a third. Most interesting was an old wooden cabinet that turned out to be full of trays of glittering beetles, all carefully mounted with pins.

There were lots of books, too, serious-looking books about the environment by Rachel Carson and Edward O. Wilson, and picture books, especially about bugs.

One whole wall was shelves. Willa went closer and saw:

tree branches with silvery green moss
dried leaves and ferns
feathers, tiny down ones as well as a big black feather, maybe from a crow
stones
snail shells
birds' nests, large and small
animal skulls!

Willa studied science in school, but it didn't interest her all that much. She dutifully went to the library or looked up information on the computer about class projects, like "Geckos." She would copy out bits of information and stick them into her papers: "The gecko generally lives in tropical regions. It is one of the only lizards to make noise. It can walk on walls or ceilings or glass due to the special pads on its feet."

But those were just facts in the encyclopedia. Willa had never seen a real gecko.

The times she'd visited Papa and Cindi in San Diego, they'd gone to the big zoo there, and that was fun, of course. But the animals were in cages or off in the re-created natural habitats and, although they were strange and wonderful (she liked the giraffes a lot), they never seemed quite real to Willa. In Chicago she'd gone to the Field Museum of Natural History with her class, but the things she'd seen there were all mixed up with laughing and running and getting into trouble and being lectured. It was all mixed up with Emma, and Willa could hardly remember what they'd been supposed to learn or look at.

All the things in Janie's room seemed very real—real and ordinary and more than a little amazing. She picked up the stones on the shelves and touched the nests with her index finger. She smelled the snail shells and rubbed a piece of bark on her hand and smoothed a feather on her cheek.

She looked at the labels. It suddenly struck Willa as astonishing that all the objects on the shelves had a place in the natural world, and all of them had names.

People had given them names, and people remembered the names and wrote them down, and that's what Janie had done, too.

teal egg
mayfly
great diving beetle
pintail feather
water starwort

There was a kind of poetry here, poetry in the words and beauty in the things themselves. So many things!

Something inside a bag on the floor moved, and Willa jumped.

"Meow?" the small gray cat said inquisitively, and slowly stretched and came toward her.

Willa crouched down and petted the little creature.

"That's Rain," said Janie sleepily, coming into the room. She was wearing a big, billowing flannel nightgown, which made Willa feel better about being in pj's. "We found her on the front porch one day in a grocery bag we'd left outside. You've heard of the Cat in the Hat? She's the Cat in the Bag."

Willa kept petting Rain, and sneaked a look at Janie. She guessed she could get used to the way Janie looked, but she couldn't help wondering what her mother would say—about Janie's colorful hair as well as this room, which was such a wonderful mess.

"It's pretty cool in here," said Willa.

Janie smiled, a wide friendly smile, and her green eyes sparkled. "What do you like to read, Willa?"

"I like mysteries," said Willa. "But not the gory ones. My brother reads stuff like that. I like *Harriet the Spy,* where she follows people and sees what they do." Willa checked her enthusiasm. She didn't want Janie thinking she was the kind of person who would go around spying on them.

"I loved *Harriet the Spy,*" said Janie, sitting down on the floor next to her. "And I agree, I don't really like those bloody mysteries. I like scientific sleuthing."

"Scientific sleuthing?"

"Detection! Asking questions. Getting answers." She pointed to some books on the shelves about Louis Pasteur and Marie Curie. "All the great scientists were private eyes. They wondered. They watched. They waited. And because they asked the right kind of questions and paid attention, they solved important puzzles and sometimes cured serious diseases."

Rain made a dash at Janie's full nightgown and lost herself in its folds.

"Breakfast," Janie decided, "and then a day full of adventures."

"Maybe some detection?" asked Willa hopefully.

"The mysteries of the universe await us! Meet me downstairs in ten."

Chapter 5

The first thing they did that day was pick up Tabby. Aunt Carmen came to the door in a velvet bathrobe the color of crushed grapes. Her thick black hair was piled on her head and she had on lots of eye makeup. She'd been practicing her role as the Duchess of Berwick in the play *Lady Windermere's Fan,* and yawned as she drawled in an English accent, "My dears, you're up early today. Are you looking for my youngest daughter? You'll find her in the garden. The servants will show you the way."

The grand effect was slightly marred by the fact that Aunt Carmen had on fluffy bedroom slippers in the shape of two squirrels.

Yesterday the sky had been gray, but this morning the sunshine glistened off the dark evergreens at the back of the yard. There was a tree of some kind with hard fruit buds attached to twigs like decorations, and several roses were climbing in yellow and pink clusters up one fence. Under the tree, a picnic table, benches, and a couple of aluminum chairs rose out of the tall grass. A typical backyard in summer. What wasn't so typical were the large, rectangular wooden boxes on the ground with a path of bark chips in between them.

These long rectangles looked like sandboxes, but they were filled with dark brown earth and lots of green. All Willa recognized were some lettuce heads. And maybe the broccoli, now that she went closer, but Willa had never seen broccoli except as little green florets that sometimes came on salads and that you could push to the side. These broccoli bunches were big and so dark they were almost blue black, and they were were sticking all over a plant four feet tall. The plant could almost be from another planet.

In the middle of the bark path, Tabby was holding a hose, doing her morning watering. She had on shorts and a T-shirt. Her feet were bare and splashed with water and dirt. As Janie and Willa walked over, she gave them a smile that showed her dimple.

"My slug trap is working," she said.

She pointed to a plastic bottle that was filled with slimy mush and pinkish orange chunks.

"You were right, Janie," said Tabby. "They love cat food. They go right through the opening and eat and then they're trapped. The little devils!" She shook the bottle. "That'll teach you to eat my lettuce."

"Can't you just poison them?" Willa asked.

"Use pesticides? No way!"

"Why not?" asked Willa.

"There's no doubt about it," said Janie. "Pesticides *work.* Or at least they used to work, before the bugs started getting tougher. Most farmers still use them though, and lots of homeowners. "

"But not us!" said Tabby. "We had a program in school. The weed killers and insect killers get into the streams in Seattle, and can kill the salmon."

"That's right," said Janie. "Herbicides and insect sprays can pollute the streams that feed into Puget Sound. Pesticides kill wildlife, too, especially birds."

Janie's voice was so kind that Willa couldn't really feel embarrassed. All the same she thought, Well, how am I supposed to know? Willa remembered that her teacher in school had sometimes talked about pollution in the Great Lakes, but she'd always made it sound like things had gotten lots better. She told the class that the rivers and lakes around Chicago and

Detroit and Cincinnati used to be so dirty that all the fish died, and the water had so much oil in it that it even caught on fire. Willa remembered seeing a picture of a river on fire.

Like Janie and Tabby, Emma was a kind of environmentalist, Willa supposed. She belonged to the World Wildlife Fund and had a poster of a panda in her bedroom. When she saw women on the street wearing any kind of fur except fake, Emma got upset.

Tabby was busy showing them all around. When she touched the broccoli, it was with a gentle pat, as if she was really fond of it. Here and there, among the carrots and beans and tomato plants, were colored envelopes that Willa recognized as seed packets. Some old, faint memory from California came back to her. She was in the backyard planting snapdragon seeds. Her mother had given her the packet, telling her, "When I was a little girl growing up in the Midwest, we had a big garden every summer. Snapdragons were my favorite flower. It might be too hot for them here."

It probably had been too hot. Willa didn't remember the snapdragons in flower, only some dry, cracked earth and brown, broken stalks.

Janie was saying, "More and more people are realizing it makes sense to farm organically, because we have to eat and drink whatever poison we put into the earth."

Willa wandered over to the roses and buried her face in one of the largest yellow ones. She felt sad, but it wasn't a bad sadness. She liked to remember good things about the time in California, about her parents and life then. It was when she couldn't remember, when she got confused about the past, or when she only remembered shouting and doors slamming that her stomach hurt. Words could be a kind of poison, too.

Aunt Carmen came out onto the back porch. She'd changed from her bathrobe and slippers into a long skirt and a sweater. On her head was a huge sweeping hat with an ostrich feather curling on it. Holding her thick coffee mug like a delicate teacup, she crooked her little finger and recited some lines from the play. "Ah, the dear pretty baby! How is the little darling? Is it a boy or a girl? I hope a girl—ah, no, I remember it's a boy! I'm so sorry. Boys are so wicked."

Shoulders back, Aunt Carmen swept down the short flight of stairs from the porch to the grass. There she seated herself gracefully on one of the lawn chairs.

Janie clapped and Willa smiled. She *liked* Aunt Carmen. But she caught a glimpse of Tabby's face and realized that Tabby was watching Willa to see if she thought her mother was just too much. Willa poked Tabby in the ribs and said, "Boys are so wicked," and the two of them cracked up. Tabby wasn't Emma; maybe she was something better, not just a friend, but family.

Their first adventure that day was the construction site where Aunt Ceci was working to help build a new high school. After the quiet of Tabby's garden, the construction site was like an earthquake and a three-ring circus all in one. Everywhere you looked were earth-moving machines and cranes and men shouting.

Ceci met them at the gate. She had on jeans and a T-shirt, an orange vest, and thick-soled boots caked with dirt and dried cement. On her head was a big, yellow plastic hat like a football helmet but with a brim. Low around her waist she wore a wide leather belt with pouches and loops for different tools. Two hammers, a screwdriver, and a tape measure hung down from her belt. How heavy it must be for the workers to carry all those tools on their hips, Willa thought.

They couldn't go inside the huge chain-link fence that circled the block because it was something called a "hard-hat area." Both Tabby and Willa laughed; it did look funny to see everybody going around in round yellow hats like some species of beetle. But Aunt Ceci said it was all part of the safety procedures required now in construction.

Aunt Ceci took off her tool belt and hat. Her curly black hair was dusty and matted. Janie fluffed it up a little and they hugged. Aunt Ceci was on her lunch break. The workers ate lunch early because they started work early and got off early. Willa wanted to know why.

"Because we know that the neighbors like to wake up to the sound of hammers and saws!" Aunt Ceci joked.

They walked around the outside of the site while Aunt Ceci ate her peanut butter sandwich and apple and cookies. They all ate cookies, in fact.

Living in Chicago, Willa had seen a lot of buildings going up, but usually they were all wrapped up in scaffolding and you had to walk through wooden tunnels built over the sidewalk to protect you from falling things. You couldn't look up and see what was going on.

Here you could see everything. There was a big hole in the ground where cement had been poured over thick twists of metal called rebar. That was the foundation, Aunt Ceci said. What she did was hammer together wood to make forms, and then the concrete was poured into the forms. The construction started at the foundation, and then went up from there. Because this was a school, it would only have four stories, but Aunt Ceci had worked on buildings that were twenty stories tall.

Willa looked in awe at how large the project was. "When I heard you were a carpenter," she told her aunt, "I always pictured you building houses."

"There are all kinds of carpenters," said Aunt Ceci. "Some make cabinets, some install doors and windows, some remodel houses. When I started out, I thought I'd be building houses. I have built a couple. But mostly I work on big jobs like this. I don't mind the heights. You get a great view up there." She pointed at a huge crane that was standing nearby. "That tower crane will lift all the heavy material to the workers, as we go up, floor by floor."

Tabby was interested, but she couldn't help saying, "It's so *ugly* here, Aunt Ceci. With the earth all ripped up, and all the trucks and port-o-potties, and this big old fence."

They were walking by a stand of trees that the fence skirted. A small stream ran through the trees and then came out again into the job site. Around the construction area many of the trees were cut down, and the stream looked muddy.

"It's not really ugly," Aunt Ceci said. "It's a work in progress. When the building is finished, they'll plant more trees and lots of grass and shrubs. And everybody will appreciate the stream."

Janie said, in a lowered voice, "I hope nobody is dumping anything in this section of the stream."

"Oh, no," said Aunt Ceci quickly. "This is a good company. They're very environmentally conscious. Not like the one I worked for last year."

"I hope so," said Janie, and they dropped the subject. But Willa felt curious. Was there a mystery here?

"Don't you always work for the same company, Aunt Ceci?" Willa asked. They were walking back to the front gate now.

"No," Aunt Ceci said. "I work with the carpenters' union. That means they send me out on different jobs. I don't have to take the jobs, but it's not good if you refuse too much. Then they don't call you back."

Willa filed this information away. This was a different kind of work than she'd seen before. Her mother had worked for American Gypsum for six years, and Willa didn't even really know what she did. Her father had his own real estate office in a strip mall. Neither of them belonged to a union, though

Willa had once heard her father say that the unions were too powerful.

"Are you the only girl here?" Tabby's sharp eyes had been surveying the groups of workers sitting and standing around the foundation. Everyone was starting to gather together again. Willa couldn't see any women. There were African Americans and Latinos, but most of the workers were white men, some with beards and long hair tied back, most of them wearing jeans and boots and heavy tool belts.

"No," said Aunt Ceci, "there are three of us on this job." She laughed to see their frowning faces. "That's a lot! I've been on plenty of jobs where I'm the only woman. Or there will be a few women laborers, but no journeymen carpenters."

What a funny expression. "Journeymen . . . ," Willa started to ask, but Janie gently tugged on her arm.

"Ceci has to get back to work. We'll see her later tonight, and she can tell you more."

"Thanks for stopping by," said Aunt Ceci, sticking her hard hat back on and strapping her weighty tool belt back around her hips. She strode toward the group of men. As she got closer to them, she seemed to get smaller and smaller. Next to some of the guys she looked very small indeed.

Chapter 6

Janie took them out for lunch to a tiny, bustling place called the Red Mill. Tabby ordered a Gardenburger. Not Willa. She heard her father's voice saying, "I'm a red meat man." She was a red meat girl, and she loved hamburgers and fries.

But she asked if she could taste the Gardenburger, and to her surprise it was pretty good. She'd thought it would be mashed broccoli or something.

After they'd eaten, Jane pulled two cloth bags out of her knapsack and asked Tabby and Willa to look inside. They each took out a blocky journal with smooth blank pages, a magnifying glass, a pen and pencil, and a handful of colored pencils.

"These are your field journals," said Janie, "kind of a combination artist sketchbook and scientific tool."

"Oh good," said Tabby. "I love to draw."

But Willa was worried. She had liked to draw—once—but it had been a long time since she'd tried. The science part made her a little nervous, too. "Scientific sleuthing" sounded fun, but what if it was really about memorization and writing down facts?

Facts were only interesting when you could make them a little more dramatic. That's why she liked writing in the private diary she already had. This one seemed more like a school project. Still, she thanked Janie. The journal had nice oatmeal-colored paper and a good square feel.

They got back into the car and drove to Salmon Creek Park, where Janie worked as an environmental educator.

It was a wilder park than Willa had seen before. Her favorite park in Chicago had green lawns shaded by oaks and maples. This was more of a dark forest of tall evergreens woven with cascades of shimmering, bright green leaves. Shafts of light, some hardly as wide as a flashlight beam, lit up a fallen tree here and a flicker of water there.

They had the car windows open and everything smelled fresh, like a Christmas tree lot, but in summer. Willa was full of wonder, but a little nervous, too. They were so tall, so dark, so ancient, these woods.

They drove up to a clearing and a small building. That was the park's nature center, where Janie planned school programs and made exhibits and organized nature walks on weekends.

Willa hadn't quite been able to imagine Janie's job as an environmental educator, but seeing the building where she worked made it easier. The downstairs was like a schoolroom, with long tables along the walls and displays of objects found in the park. Most were labeled in the handwriting Willa had seen in Janie's office at home: *eagle feather, salmon eggs.* The word *watershed* was written everywhere. The whole park was in something called the Salmon Creek Watershed. It made Willa think of a raincoat advertisement.

"I need to go upstairs and check my messages," said Janie.

"Can we go explore?" asked Tabby, jumping up and down.

"Sure. Why don't you show Willa the beach? I'll meet you there. And take your new bags and field journals!"

Willa's face must have looked a little anxious, because Janie said, "It's not far to the beach, Willa. But if you'd rather wait for me . . ."

"Come *on,* Willa. Race you!"

Willa thought, well, if *Tabby* isn't scared to go through the woods . . . and off they went. They ran along the side of the road until they were out of breath. Running was good. Running always felt good. That was something Willa had forgotten lately.

The road led up a hill to a playground with a huge slide shaped like a fish and swings and picnic tables. They ran through it and over a bridge that crossed train tracks. The ocean spread out in front of them as they pelted down the stairs to the sand. Only it wasn't the ocean, it was Puget Sound, Tabby said. The sound was indigo blue with splashes of white, and in the distance a bulky white ship chugged across. Tabby called it a ferry.

Tabby threw off her shoes as soon as she got to the beach, even though it was rocky as well as sandy. She had such *long* brown legs, thought Willa, feeling stumpy and pale. Usually at the end of summer, especially after going to San Diego, she'd be tan. But she'd never be able to match Tabby's beautiful light chocolate color.

Tabby had clambered over the stony part of the beach to the smooth sand by the water and was already wet up to her ankles. Willa hadn't exactly thought of Tabby as a quiet girl, but, maybe because of her glasses, she'd seemed more dignified than she really was.

Because now she was whooping and carrying on in the waves like a wild thing.

And Willa joined her.

They weren't completely soaked when Janie found them a short while later, but they were *pretty* wet.

Their cloth bags with the field journals and pencils had been carelessly tossed on the shore, along with their shoes.

Janie looked disappointed for a minute, the way grown-ups do when they hope you'll choose the educational toy or film, and instead you choose the fun, no-brainer thing to do. But then she ran to join them in the waves. With her pants rolled up above her knees and her bright hair glinting in the sun, she looked like another kid.

And she got pretty wet, too.

Later, the three of them lay drying off on the large granite rocks.

"The man next to me on the plane said it was always cold and rainy here in the summer," observed Willa, luxuriously letting the sand run through her fingers. "Boy, was he wrong."

Janie laughed. "Well, not every day is going to be a nice one. It's a maritime climate. But I love even the gray days in the Northwest."

"What are the summers like where you're from, Willa?" asked Tabby.

"Hot! Over a hundred sometimes. And we have thunderstorms. Most years I've gone to camp with my friend Emma, and we swim as much as we can to stay cool, or sit under trees. You just get too hot to move."

"I'd like to go to Chicago," said Tabby. "I like to be hot."

Willa thought, if Tabby was with me at camp, I wouldn't mind about Emma and Parker.

Tabby picked up her field journal and a pencil and started to draw a piece of dried seaweed wrapped around a speckled stone.

When she finished, she wrote GRANITE in large letters. "I don't know the kind of seaweed, though," she said.

"I don't know the name either," said Janie.

Does seaweed have more than one name? thought Willa.

Janie picked up a small fragment of brown crackly seaweed from another rock and popped it into her mouth.

"Euw!" said Tabby.

"It's good for you! Lots of vitamins and minerals, iodine too. Try it, Willa."

"It's not poisonous?"

"No, but that's a good question. Read up or ask before you chew. I know that the coastal Indians around Puget Sound used seaweed for all kinds of things. They made soup with it, they wrapped fish in it and baked it."

The three of them munched.

"It's not bad," said Willa, "salty."

She looked out at the water and breathed deeply the smell of sun and sand and seaweed. "You have a great job, I think," she said to Janie, "being outside like this all the time."

"It *is* a good job," said Janie, and then paused. "It's not your typical forty-hour-a-week occupation though. The park is funded by the city, so they cut my hours back in the summer when there are no school groups coming through. In the summer I work a lot, too, but don't get paid as much."

"That's like my mom," said Tabby. "She works by doing plays, but she doesn't get paid very much."

"Some things you do because you love them," said Janie.

Willa knew that her father loved to sell houses, but she wasn't so sure her mother liked being an executive.

What will I find to do in life? Willa wondered.

A seagull sailed overhead and then out over the water in a graceful swoop. Watching it, every other thought left Willa's brain. She was just happy to be here.

Chapter 7

They walked back to the nature center through a scraggly looking wooded area that was partly swamp and partly running water.

This was Salmon Creek.

"It's one of the few salmon streams to empty right into Puget Sound. We've been working to restore the habitat of the creek. A lot of what you see here is new." Jane waved at the swampy area with a walkway over it.

"It looks messy," said Willa. She didn't want to hurt Janie's feelings, but if this was working to restore the creek, they had a lot of work to do. There were broken tree limbs all over the place and sticks floating in the water. The water was green with stuff growing underneath and on the surface. Blue dragonflies skimmed by, and a few ducks sailed quietly in the middle.

"Nature likes a mess," Janie said. "This is a wetland. It's neither land nor water, but something in between. It's like a giant sponge that absorbs water enough for thousands of life-forms—microscopic life-forms we can't see—and plenty of insects to eat those microscopic things, and fish and birds to eat the bugs."

"Are there alligators here?" asked Willa. When she thought of a swamp, she thought of creepy-crawly monsters.

"It's not warm enough," said Tabby. "That's the Everglades. We went to the Everglades once when we went to Disney World. Now that was some swamp!"

"A great deal of North America was covered with wetlands once," said Janie. "Beavers made the wetlands. They made dams around the rivers and creeks, and that made the water back up and spread out. But there aren't as many beavers left."

"What happened to them?" asked Willa.

"They got eaten!" said Tabby. "And that's why I'm a vegetarian today."

"No, they weren't killed to be eaten," said Janie. "They were killed for their fur. People liked to wear beaver hats in the old days."

"What's a watershed then?" Willa asked, remembered the signs she'd seen in the nature center.

"It's an area that drains into a river or stream. All of the smaller streams around here drain into Salmon Creek. But storm drains do, too."

"*Drains* go into the creek?" asked Tabby.

"Not the sewage lines, no, just the storm drains. When it rains, water flowing from the streets goes down into the drains and comes out here. Whatever people put into the street gutters comes out here too, whether it's paint or oil from their cars."

"But wouldn't that make the water in Salmon Creek all yucky for the fish?" Tabby wondered.

Janie nodded. "That's why we need to take care of the water. Because the fish can't do it themselves! I want you two to help me take some samples, okay?"

Janie brought out jam jars, and Willa and Tabby stepped gingerly down to the edge of the squishy marsh. The water they scooped up wasn't clear, but greenish brown, with strings of green and bits of moss and old leaves. A few tiny, wriggly things swam in circles, like carousel animals behind glass.

Willa heard music, as she peered inside the jam jar, but it wasn't the lively organ music of a carousel. It was a country-western song, and came from a dirt parking lot on the other side of the wetland. Through the trees and thick bushes she could see the shiny hoods of cars, the glossy cabs of trucks. Occasionally a motor would rumble; when that happened, you couldn't hear the birds.

"Guys and their cars," said Janie, shrugging, when Tabby asked. "They use that area of the park to hang out and look under their hoods. They're not supposed to make a mess or dump anything in the creek. Other than that, we can't really stop them. Kind of destroys the mood, though, doesn't it?"

Janie began to lead them out of the wetland to the path that followed the creek. The water rushed and pushed eagerly over the stones and sand.

"I don't see any fish," observed Tabby. "Where are the salmon?"

"Oh, you won't see them again until later in the year. They'll return from the sea and swim upstream to lay their eggs. After that, they die. By some amazing instinct that we don't completely understand, the salmon will find their way from the middle of the ocean back to the very same creek where they were born, years before. Do you think you could find your way back to Chicago, Willa?"

"I'd walk east," she said, trying to sound like it was no big deal. "East and east and east."

"You'd be an old lady when you got back," said Tabby.

"Just like the salmon by the time they get home to Salmon Creek," said Janie. "Speaking of home, I promised I'd get you girls back to our house around four. Your dad's going to pick you up, Tabby."

She took out another pair of jam jars, and gestured to the bank by a wooden bridge. "We'll come here again," she promised, "lots of times. But before we go, let's take samples from the creek."

The two girls scooped the jars into the quickly moving stream. Willa had been wondering if she'd see a lot of junk from the storm drains. This water wasn't even brown, but clear as rain. That made her glad, for the fish.

Chapter 8

When they arrived at the house, Willa felt suddenly shy, just as she had yesterday at the airport. In the backyard under the plum tree, sat Uncle James, the image of calm, and Phyllis, cool and confident in white shorts and a big red T-shirt. Aunt Ceci was home from work and fresh from the shower. Her black hair was still wet, and just starting to form ringlets around her round cheeks.

Willa felt hot and uncomfortable. Her clothes were still damp and bits of gritty sand scraped her inside her shorts and sneakers.

"Look at my field journal. Look at my picture," said Tabby excitedly. She threw herself on her father, who laughed and hugged her and exclaimed over the granite stone with seaweed.

Something about this made Willa feel as if gritty sand had gotten into her throat as well as her clothes. *She* didn't have a picture to show.

And she didn't have a father. At least, not one who was around to hug her.

Aunt Ceci must have seen something in Willa's face, because she got up and said, "How about a shower, Willa? And then let's call your mom. She left a message for you today."

"She did?"

All of a sudden Willa felt much better.

In the shower Willa imagined a long conversation with her mother. She told her everything that had happened since she came. It seemed a lot longer than just one day.

". . . And we went swimming in Puget Sound, and Janie gave me and Tabby field journals to keep notes. And we saw where Aunt Ceci works. She's building a new high school. She wears a hard hat! And Aunt Carmen is in a play. She's a duchess."

"Well, that figures," Willa's mom would laugh. "I'm glad you're having such a great time. It seems *very* quiet around here without you kids. You know I love you very much."

But when Willa tried calling her mother, there was no answer. Willa left a message, then she went upstairs to her room. She couldn't quite face everybody out in the backyard asking about her mother.

Janie was in her office. She took one look at Willa and didn't ask. She only said, cheerfully, "We'll try again later."

Then she beckoned Willa in. The room was even more chaotic than earlier, since Janie had moved some piles of paper from the table to the floor to make room for the microscope and the jars of water from Salmon Creek Park.

"Let's have a look at the water from the wetland and then from the creek," Janie invited, patting the stool next to her.

In spite of her homesickness, Willa was interested. She'd seen pictures of scientists in lab coats with their heads bent over microscopes, but she had never been sure exactly what they were looking at. In seventh grade, in the fall, she'd have some kind of beginning biology class, but so far in school she'd just done simple experiments, without a lot of equipment.

"First, you take a slide," said Janie, pulling a box of small glass rectangles toward her. She set an eyedropper in front of Willa. "It's easy. Just open the jar and get some water, then put a drop on the slide. We can put a clear plastic slide cover over the drop to flatten it, or just look at it as it is. Let's do that."

Willa opened the jar of greenish brown water and sucked a little up into the dropper. Then she placed a drop on the slide under the lens of the microscope.

"Now you turn the turret of the microscope around to find the right lens. You tilt the reflector so the light comes up in the right direction. Then you take a look."

With her face down to the eyepiece, Janie screwed the magnification knob a few times and then motioned Willa to look. First there was just a blurry bright gray nothingness, and then there was a tiny bit of movement and some fast little shapes came into focus.

It seemed as though they were paddling around in a large swimming pool, and it was hard to remember this was a just tiny drop of water. There were round shapes that bounced like beach balls, and smaller shapes more like teardrops with a tiny tail. Janie said these were probably paramecia—single-celled animals.

Animals!

The water drop from the wetland held lots of shapes and lines and moving parts. But when Willa opened the jar of creek water and placed a drop on another slide, there was little to be seen, only a shiny orb of light with a few vague lines. It was just what Janie had said: life was more abundant where the water was warm and still, not cool and moving.

Willa made a new slide of wetland water. She bent her head and looked again, fiddling with the knob to bring the shapes into focus. This time she noticed even more tiny things. They were wriggling and somersaulting and gliding like dancers. Watching them, Willa began to experience a most peculiar feeling.

This water was alive.

It wasn't just that water was some *thing* that had wriggly *things* in it; it was that the water itself was vibrating and shivering with life.

She pulled back slowly from the eyepiece; her heart was beating quickly. Willa felt as though she'd just, for a fragment of a second, seen into the heart of the universe.

She looked at Janie.

"Yes," said Janie, smiling. "It can take your breath away, can't it?"

Willa blinked. Everything in the room looked big and solid after the mystery of the gleaming, moving drop of water. "It reminds me," she said, "of a program I once watched on TV about ballroom dancing. The camera was shooting the dancers from above, so they were these beautiful shapes moving in a circle. Does that make sense, that it looks like ballroom dancing?"

"When you look at things very hard, you go past observation into some other world," said Janie. "Science merges with imagination."

That was the picture Willa was left with as she and Janie went downstairs: paramecium in fancy dress, waltzing around a glowing ballroom with a glass floor.

Chapter 9

Back outside, under the plum tree, Uncle James and Aunt Ceci were drinking lemonade and talking about unions. Aunt Ceci was saying that she'd been noticing more and more nonunion jobs around town, and that some carpenters she met didn't even want to join the union.

"I used to feel that way," said Uncle James. "Why try to join the electrician's union, when it was clear they didn't want black people around?"

In a corner of the garden Tabby was thinning Janie's carrots, pulling out orange stubs half the size of her finger. Phyllis had stretched her big, strong body out on the grass in the warm afternoon sun.

"I remember that your union wasn't very welcoming to women either," said Aunt Ceci. "A friend of mine had real problems with the guys."

"No, ma'am," said Uncle James. "You recall it rightly. But they've changed. After we sat on their heads for a few years."

He laughed at Willa's expression. "I can see you're having trouble imagining that. Don't worry. It was only in spirit."

"Well, the United *Brother*-hood of Carpenters could use a little shaking up," said Aunt Ceci. "It's a lot better than twenty years ago, when I started, but it's still no paradise for women out there on the job."

Willa had gotten curious. "Aunt Ceci, how did you get to be a carpenter?"

Aunt Ceci made room for Willa next to her at the table. "Well, I was a girl who liked to make things, first of all—boxes, little tables, picture frames. The neighbor next door was a woodworker in his spare time and had a great little shop in his basement. Your papa and I used to go over there sometimes on weekends and he'd let us hammer nails to our hearts' content."

Aunt Ceci smiled, remembering. "This guy, Louie, was great. He taught me to measure and to saw and even to use an electric drill. But he never suggested that I could be a carpenter when I grew up, because girls just don't do that kind of thing—or at least that's what they used to think. So when I got older I went to college and got a degree in English. I had no idea what to do with it, of course. I wandered up the West Coast, from San Diego to Seattle, where I found my sister Carmen had married a very nice guy called James."

While Aunt Ceci was telling her story, Tabby had come over and sat next to her father. Uncle James had a big smile on his face. He said, "So here came Carmen's little sister. She was little, but she was strong. She had wild curly hair—it was long then!—and she said she'd been making a living doing odd jobs. She wasn't afraid of sharp things. Or heights!"

"James was an electrician and knew about construction. He told me, Try it! The worst that can happen is that they'll ignore you when you go asking for a job."

Now Phyllis was listening too. "I would hate that," she said decisively, "I get so *mad* when people ignore me."

"I got mad, too," said Aunt Ceci. "But the more I saw of construction, the more I wanted to do it. After a while, they got used to me turning up on jobs, and someone gave me a job picking up after the carpenters. I found out the union had an apprenticeship program and managed to get into that. Then they *had* to take me more seriously on the building sites."

Aunt Ceci looked up at the plum tree as if she was

imagining climbing scaffolding. "To make a long story short, after a few years of taking classes and learning on the job, and learning to keep my mouth shut at the right time and not kill myself or anybody else, I finally became a full-fledged carpenter, what they call a journeyman or journey-level carpenter. And I wasn't the only one. There were other women who made it through the system, too."

Tabby had found a marble in the dirt while she'd been weeding and thinning. She rolled it in her hand and said, thoughtfully, "Then why are there only three women on your job? And there were only two black men. I counted."

"Sometimes there are lots more," said Aunt Ceci quickly. Then she laughed, "You got me Tabby. I want to give you girls hope, but the reality is still tough."

Uncle James said, "We've come a long way, but we've still got some ways to go."

"Amen, brother," said Phyllis cheekily, jumping up. "We've got some ways to go home, too, so let's saddle up those mules and get moving. Anthony's supposed to call me at six, and I want to be home."

"Her boyfriend—she wishes," explained Tabby, rolling her eyes. "An-thony, Ant-honey, that's all we ever hear now. You used to hang out with Tran. Now the two of you just want to be around *boys.*"

Phyllis lazily swatted at her and missed. "Anthony and I are going to a concert with Tran and Nyugen." She looked very pleased with herself.

What a difference a few years made, thought Willa. If Phyllis had a boyfriend, would she be interested in hanging out with Tabby and Willa? Willa wanted to get to know her older cousin, but she was a little afraid of her, too. She was so big and smart and certain of herself.

Willa's mother called just after dinner. Her voice sounded bright and excited. She'd just come home from the first meeting of her new book club. They were going to get together all summer, every two weeks, to discuss books they were reading. Willa didn't like the sound of it—too much like school—but her mother seemed thrilled. "What a great bunch of people they are. They've been meeting for years. I'm so lucky there was an opening for me!"

It seemed strange to Willa that she and her mother had been together yesterday morning in Chicago, and that today she'd seen and done so many things. She'd been on a building site. She'd splashed in Puget Sound. She'd learned about pesticides and wetlands. She'd looked through a microscope. She hadn't drawn anything yet in her new field journal, but she would! She'd make it like a detective diary; she'd be a scientific sleuth.

Willa had done so much, in fact, that it was funny when her mom asked, "Do you think you'll find enough to keep you busy this summer?"

All the same, Willa felt a little sad when she said good night to Janie and Aunt Ceci and went up the steep, narrow stairs to her bedroom. She hadn't returned the brown fleece vest to her aunt, and now she put it on and snuggled into its softness and its faint scent of lavender and sawdust.

Chapter 10

The summer days passed. Mornings when Willa woke in the cozy, slant-ceiling room upstairs, she often had a quick flash that things were different here. The light came earlier and the birds were louder. When she went downstairs, she could step right outside into the backyard.

At home she didn't go outside just to be outside, at least not to run her toes through the grass. There was usually a purpose to going outdoors. It meant she was on the way to or from the school bus, or shopping, or a movie. In the winter it was too cold and in the summer it was too hot. There were lots of things she loved about living in a big city. When they rode the elevated train she loved to see the busy neighborhoods and tall buildings. Downtown

Chicago was an exciting place to be. But except for the lake, it wasn't a very outdoorsy sort of place. Even when they went to the lake, it didn't seem very wild, though it was definitely fun to play in the water and make sandcastles and eat ice cream.

For the last few years, Willa had gone to camp with Emma. That was for sure an outdoors experience. But even in upstate Michigan, in the wilderness, everybody always seemed in a big hurry, the counselors as well as the kids. It was a rush to get up in the morning and to get to swimming or canoeing lessons. If a counselor ever saw you just *sitting* somewhere, doing nothing, just *looking* at a tree or a bird, she would ask you where you were supposed to be, or start making suggestions for what you could do. Even worse, she might get a concerned expression on her face and ask if you were homesick.

It was different here in Janie and Aunt Ceci's backyard. Willa could go and look at the chickadees and finches in the plum tree and play with Rain the cat, and see if the squash seeds she'd planted were coming up yet. There were lots of things to do during the day, but Willa didn't feel rushed. Janie and Aunt Ceci were not rushed kind of people, not like Willa's mom.

Yes, life in Seattle seemed different, Willa thought. It was greener and wilder. It was smaller too, and quieter. Even though the downtown had plenty of skyscrapers and the traffic was terrible, it didn't have the bustle and energy of Chicago. It didn't have the pizzazz either. But all the same, she felt more at home in Seattle every day.

She saw a lot of Tabby. One very warm day (Willa refused to say it was actually *hot*), they went swimming at an open-air pool right next to Puget Sound. Another day they worked in Janie and Aunt Ceci's garden for a couple of hours, pulling weeds and spraying aphids with soapy water. Afterward Tabby made broccoli and cheese quiche for lunch. Willa couldn't believe how good Tabby was at rolling out the pie dough. They made chocolate chip cookies, too, and that was something Willa was good at.

With Janie, they looked through the microscope at the skin of an onion, a hair from each of their heads, and a leaf. The leaf looked as if it was an oval box full of shining green bubbles. When you knew this was how the world was put together, from a gazillion tiny cells, you couldn't look at it the same way. As Tabby said, after seeing the leaf, "I'm blind with amazement!" It was what her grandmother, her father's mother, used to say. Now Willa knew exactly what Tabby's grandmother had meant.

One afternoon they went with Aunt Carmen to a

rehearsal for *Lady Windermere's Fan.* It took place in an old building that used to be a neighborhood movie theater. The seats were worn plush, and everything had a dusty, musty smell. All the actors were normal-looking people when they arrived, wearing shorts and T-shirts, but a few of them brought top hats or feather boas. One man wore a monocle, a piece of round glass scrunched up in one eye. The boas and top hats looked very funny with T-shirts that said *Northwest Folklife Festival* and *Save the Rainforest.*

All of them spoke in normal voices, until they got up on stage and started trying to talk like they were British.

Pete, the director, was a tubby young man whose hair was so thin on top that it looked like he'd pulled most of it out in frustration. He would call out, "This isn't Malibu Beach, Patty, and you're not waltzing along in a bathing suit. You're Lady Plymdale walking into a London drawing room. You're wearing a *corset.* You're an aristocat!"

Willa found the plot confusing. Lady Windermere thought that Mrs. Erlynne was Lord Windermere's girlfriend, but it turned out Mrs. Erlynne was Lady Windermere's *mother,* who had abandoned her when she was a baby. It seemed like even the actors couldn't quite believe it. The man who played Lord Darlington was a very cool guy. He and Aunt Carmen, as the Duchess of Berwick, knew their lines and seemed to be having fun tossing the words back and forth as though they were tennis balls. Hardly anybody else got to say more than a few lines before the director was telling them they were saying it all wrong or moving all wrong. Willa thought she would fall apart if somebody shouted at her the way Pete was shouting at everybody, but none of the cast seemed to think it was strange at all.

"Oh, Pete always sounds like he's having a nervous breakdown," said Aunt Carmen when she joined them after the rehearsal.

She called out to Pete, who was mopping his forehead with a handkerchief and muttering over his notes, "Thanks for letting the girls come. I don't think they'd ever seen a grown man cry like that before."

"You're lucky I didn't have a full-fledged tantrum and fall to the floor and scream and kick," he said and gave them a wink.

"Maybe next time," said Tabby.

Wherever Aunt Carmen was, was excitement. Janie and Aunt Ceci provided excitement of a different kind. From Aunt Ceci, Willa was learning to make birdhouses. Not that Aunt Ceci would let her run the power tools in her shop in the basement, but after Aunt Ceci had cut the pieces of wood, Willa learned the right way to hammer them together.

It was harder than it looked. The nails could bend so easily. They could poke through the wood in the wrong direction. And you could smash your thumb hammering. Willa's left thumbnail was blue for a week.

But, after making some mistakes, Willa managed to construct a four-sided box with a pointed roof. Aunt Ceci drilled two holes in it: one about an inch wide for the opening and the other to attach a tiny dowel for a perch. Afterwards Willa painted it green, and put an address over the entrance. She hung it out behind Aunt Ceci's workshop, out of reach of the neighborhood cats.

From Janie, Willa was learning that nature gets more and more interesting the more you pay attention. At Salmon Creek Park, Willa was learning to stand quietly and observe everything, from the ducks swimming in the wetland pond to the swish the trees made overhead in the wind. She wasn't much used to standing completely still, but she was getting good at it.

The only thing that Willa didn't like about the park was that the wetland was near the small lot where the guys parked their cars and trucks. She couldn't figure out what they did there. They just seemed to rev their motors and crank up their music. Not that Willa didn't like music, but it was hard to hear the sounds of nature sometimes.

"I know, I know," said Janie. "But in addition to being an environmental park in Seattle, this is a public park. And people have different ideas about what they want to do in parks. I used to work up in the North Cascades National Park. There, if people were being loud in the campground, I could go up and talk to them about it. Here, we just try to stop people from destroying things."

Willa's field journal was beginning to fill with notes and pictures. She discovered that she liked drawing maps, and that was a good way for her to remember a place. She drew a map of the stream from the entrance of the park to where it flowed out under the railroad tracks to the ocean. From a book Janie had in her office, she copied a diagram of the water cycle: how water evaporated from the ocean and became clouds and then rained down again on everything. She made lists of things she found in the creek and on the beach. She borrowed Janie's bird book, and now she could tell some of the birds apart. Janie said there were about a hundred species at the park.

Tabby's journal was very different. She liked to draw detailed objects: a twig, a flower, a rock. Everything in Willa's was on a larger scale. When she made a map, she put everything in: the clouds, the part of the stream where the bottom was gravel and sand, the flight of ducks on and off their pond.

"We should find you a project," said Janie, after a week or so, as they sat together in Janie's office at home, "Something you can sink you teeth into and really follow for a while."

In school when their teacher said "project," they all groaned. Projects were always extra work at the library.

Willa was cautious. "What kind of project?"

"Well, what interests you most?"

Willa thought. The pair of bald eagles she'd seen were really cool, and so were the funny black coots with their red eyes, and the green-breasted mallards. Something about the idea of nests appealed to her. The bald eagle nest was about as huge as a large arm-chair. Then again, she could study trees. She could try to learn something about the old-growth forests of the Northwest. Or, what about wildflowers? She could make a scrapbook and label all the specimens. Then when she got home to Chicago, she could look at it and remember.

Willa looked around. As usual, Janie's office was jammed with nature samples and with books and papers and half-constructed posterboard displays. On the big table were the microscope and various vials and bottles of water.

Willa suddenly remembered the day when she first realized water was so active, when she went beyond understanding that there were things invisible to the eye wriggling around in a drop of water.

When she'd understood that water was *alive*.

"Water," she said to Janie. "I'd like to do a water project." She remembered what they'd talked about at Aunt Ceci's construction site. Willa suggested, "Maybe we could see if the stream running near the new high school is still all right. We could be detectives. We could monitor the water quality."

Janie was always talking about "monitoring the water quality." It sounded very official.

"That's a great idea, Willa," said Janie.

But Aunt Ceci didn't look as pleased when they told her. "But why? Taylor Construction has a good environmental track record. They monitor everything. They bag up waste, and have aboveground storage tanks. They don't allow seepage. They'd never dump anything into the stream."

"But even environmentally aware companies have

workers who don't always follow the correct procedures," said Janie. "Anyway, the stream doesn't just go through the high school site. It comes from the hill above, and keeps going near the shopping mall. When you were working for Miller Construction on that office building, someone used that very same stream to dump concrete. And you noticed it and told me and I reported it."

"That was a year ago, and they paid a big fine and had to clean it up. I'm not working for that company anymore," said Aunt Ceci. "I have to say I felt bad that two workers got blamed, when I know for a fact that it was the supervisor, the owner's son, who told Bill and Andy to dump the concrete. I expected to be fired, but I was sorry they were too."

"We *each* have responsibility for our own actions," Janie began, her voice rising a little.

When Willa's parents' voices rose, they were about to start arguing. Willa interrupted, "What does concrete do to a stream? Is it poison?"

"There's lime in concrete," said Janie in her normal voice. "If it gets into the water, it changes something called the pH. The living things in the water will die if the pH isn't right."

Willa didn't quite understand, but at least Janie and Aunt Ceci were calm again.

"All I ask is that if you find something in the stream," said Aunt Ceci, "you tell me before you inform the authorities. Last year, when the inspectors came around, I looked completely guilty. I'd like to keep working with Taylor Construction. They've been decent to me, and I don't want to get a reputation as a troublemaker."

Janie said, "We can easily choose another project for Willa."

Willa suddenly understood something important. Aunt Ceci hadn't just left that old company because they were wrong to dump concrete. She'd been fired for opening her mouth.

Chapter 11

In her personal diary, Willa described the life she was living now. She wrote about Tabby and her garden, about Aunt Ceci and her carpentry tools, about Aunt Carmen and her play. Sometimes she pretended she was writing a letter to Emma. Would Emma be impressed that Willa had hammered a birdhouse together? Willa's mother was! She e-mailed Willa every other day. But so far Willa hadn't heard a word from Emma, though Willa had sent her a postcard right away.

After the talk with Janie and Aunt Ceci, Willa wrote: "I wanted to do a project about the stream near where Aunt Ceci works," wrote Willa. "But Aunt Ceci didn't think it was a good idea. I wonder if it's because she knows something about that stream???"

The more Willa thought about that, the more likely it seemed. If there was some dumping going on, it might call for some detection, some secret spying and private-eyeing.

It was at the Fourth of July picnic that Willa had her big idea.

They had gathered at Seward Park along with hundreds of other families. It wasn't the warmest weather—everybody was in sweatshirts or sweaters in the morning—but it was sunny. And in Seattle, that was something.

Everybody was there: Uncle James's brother and his family; some actor friends of Aunt Carmen's who kept falling into English accents; Phyllis and Tran and their boyfriends, Anthony and Nyugen; and Aunt Ceci and Janie and their friends Sue and Sara, whose names and faces Willa kept mixing up.

In the middle of all this, after the barbequed chicken was bones on her plate and the potato salad was a smear of mayonnaise, Willa pulled Tabby aside for a conference.

"What about—" she paused dramatically, "an adventure?"

Tabby had seen too many of her mother's rehearsals to be impressed by dramatic pauses.

"What kind of adventure?"

"A scientific adventure."

"The rainforest!"

"How could we get to Central America on our own?"

"Antarctica?" asked Tabby hopefully. "I've always wanted to see penguins."

Where did Tabby get these ideas? Willa thought.

"No, something closer to home," said Willa, and she began to explain her plan. They would go to Aunt Ceci's job site, to the stream running through it, and take water samples. Then they would mail them to some government agency and see if the construction company was telling the truth about its environmental practices.

Her brown eyes wide, Tabby asked, "Why would we want to do that?"

"Because I think Aunt Ceci suspects something, but she doesn't want to be a troublemaker and lose her job. And Janie suspects something too, but is afraid to look too closely."

Tabby still looked unconvinced. "How are we going to get there?"

"On a bus."

"How're we going to find the right bus?"

"I take buses all the time in Chicago. It's no big deal."

"Not just school buses?" Tabby looked admiringly at Willa. Willa didn't tell her that she'd never taken a bus by herself.

Then Tabby went on, "Yeah, but even if we could get to the high school on our own, there are always people working there. And when they're not working, there's a big old chain-link fence around the whole place."

"We don't have to actually go on to the job site," said Willa, trying to disguise her own worry. "The stream comes out below the site. Whatever they put in the water will wash downstream. We can go upstream, too, to the source, and take a water sample *before* it goes through the site. Then there would be two samples to compare."

"The source?" Tabby said. In spite of her caution, her eyes began to glow. "Like when they went looking for the source of the Nile? We'll be explorers!"

And with a leap, she jumped up and dashed madly across the picnic area. To the innocent eye, Tabby just looked like she was running, but Willa knew that Tabby was on her way to the banks of the Nile.

"A free spirit," Willa's mother had once called Aunt Carmen.

That's what Tabby was, too, a free spirit.

In order to carry out the *plan,* it was necessary to get Aunt Carmen's help—not with her knowledge, of course.

Willa found out from Metro Information that a bus went from Northgate Mall right by the high school construction site.

That was step one. In step two, Willa asked Aunt Carmen if she and Tabby could go to another rehearsal one afternoon. The little theater wasn't far from Northgate Mall.

Step three was to ask Aunt Carmen, once she picked Willa up, if she and Tabby could go to the mall instead.

"But I thought . . . ," Aunt Carmen began, disappointed.

"Willa wants to buy Aunt Ceci and Janie a present," Tabby improvised. "A thank-you gift."

"Well, I don't really . . . you know, the rehearsal is almost three hours long."

"Mom!" said Tabby. "The mall is totally safe. And Willa *has* to buy the present in secret."

Aunt Carmen relented. "I guess the two of you just want an adventure alone, hmm?"

Willa and Tabby nodded and tried not to look thrilled.

They found the bus without much trouble. Here,

Willa was in charge. Tabby thought Willa took buses alone all the time in the big city, and Willa now had to act like she did.

"Please let us out at . . . ," Willa asked the driver, and named the cross streets.

In her backpack she had several vials with stoppers that she'd taken from Janie's office. She could have used ordinary jars, but she'd had some idea the experiment should be sterile.

"Here's your stop," said the bus driver, and the two girls got out.

It was about four o'clock by this time. The main gate was locked and the construction site was deserted. They were lucky. Sometimes, Aunt Ceci had said, especially when there was a concrete pour, the crew stayed later. But today there was no one around.

First they took a sample from the stream coming out below the site. Willa labeled the vial with the location and date, and then Tabby led the way up the hillside above the site. In a block or two they were in a residential area where the stream ran through a ravine. At this point they left the road and entered the ravine. There was a narrow trail along the stream. Above them were houses, mostly modern looking, with decks and picture windows. Here and there a trail led upward to the street.

The ravine grew more and more lush and tangled with ferns and vines. The stream seemed to become just a trickle and to lose itself, from time to time, like a flickering silver snake in the green jungle.

With a long stick, Tabby poked and prodded at the tangled jungle they climbed through, and she talked happily about how this was a lot like the rainforest and maybe someday she and Willa would go to Central America and find the source of the Nile. Willa told her she thought the Nile was in Africa, but Tabby was not convinced.

After a while Willa began to be a little scared. It seemed as though they had gone a mile or more up the ravine. In spite of the blue sky above that told her they had hours of summer light left, Willa was uneasy. What if they weren't back at Northgate Mall when Aunt Carmen came to pick them up?

Willa had thought she'd been so smart about this plan, but she hadn't even remembered to bring a watch.

"This is interesting," Tabby was saying, poking at some leaves. "The water here is running faster and is more bubbly. I don't get it."

They bent to look. The water *was* bubbling here. It wasn't the source of the stream, but there definitely seemed to be a spring that came up from underground and joined the stream. A clear spring of water, fresh and fast, came bubbling out of the earth.

"Take the sample here," said Tabby, gently pushing aside the leaves.

Willa filled a vial and capped it with a sense of awe. It was as if they'd captured a magic elixir.

Then, right above them at the edge of the ravine, a dog began to bark fiercely, and a rough, deep voice shouted, "Get off my property!"

Chapter 12

"*His* property," Willa gasped, as they dashed back down the ravine, crashing through shrubs and grabbing at vines and expecting any minute to feel the hot breath of a mad dog on their necks. "*His* property!" she said again when they reached the street and slowed to a quick walk. "As if running water can be owned or something."

They threw themselves down on a dusty patch of grass outside the construction site. The sun was bright after the green coolness of the ravine, but even so, Tabby shivered a little. Willa realized Tabby was scared.

But Tabby said only, "That was good practice for when we're in the rainforest and meet a jaguar."

"You'd be a good explorer," said Willa. "Don't forget, we got what we went there for—the water!"

Tabby said, "Look, the bus!"

They sprinted again and the driver slowed and waited for them. It was the same driver as before. He greeted them like old friends. "Have you been running in a marathon?" he joked.

They got back to the meeting spot at the mall five minutes after the time Aunt Carmen had told them she'd meet them—and then waited another ten minutes.

"Mama is the type who's always fifteen minutes late," Tabby said philosophically. "She's never ten minutes early, never half an hour late. It's always fifteen minutes."

"My mom is always ten minutes early," said Willa. She missed her mother suddenly, even though she knew that she would never have been able to get away with this adventure at home.

Aunt Carmen arrived as the Duchess of Berwick, speaking in a grand but giddy tone to ask what they'd bought for Lady Cecilia and Dame Jane.

Willa blanked for a moment. She'd been so concerned with protecting her glass vials as she and Tabby got inside the car that she'd forgotten their cover story.

"Willa couldn't find anything right at the mall," Tabby said. "Everything is too . . . too commercial."

"No, I couldn't find anything at the mall," Willa repeated. It wasn't totally a lie. They'd found nothing at the mall because they hadn't looked at the mall.

"I'm not surprised," said the duchess. "You'd have better luck at the hardware store. Even as a small child, Lady Cecilia preferred a hammer to a doll. And as for Dame Jane, all she likes are *bugs.*"

Tabby's part in the adventure was over, but Willa had to find a way to get the vials of water tested. That evening while she was helping Janie clear off the table, she asked, "Last year, when you reported that construction company about the dumping in the stream, who did you call?"

"There's a local agency called the Surface Water Management Program. After I called them, they came out and took a sample of the water, and then they returned and did an investigation."

"But you could have taken a sample yourself and sent it to them, couldn't you?"

"I'm not sure I could have gotten away with going on the construction site with my test tubes," laughed Janie.

Aunt Ceci had been reading the newspaper in the living room. Now she came into the kitchen and asked, "Why are you so curious about all this, Willa?"

"I think it's . . . important to know stuff like this," Willa stumbled. "I mean, that people can do something to protect the environment and not just see it get trashed. So if I ever . . . saw somebody dumping something, I could say, 'Hey, that's illegal.' Then I could call the . . . Surface Water Management Program." She repeated the name, checking to see if she had it right.

"Yes, it's important to report violators," said Janie, her green eyes flashing enthusiastically, "but what we really want to do is educate people *before* they dump anything in a stream."

Janie went on, "The thing people need to realize, Willa, is that rivers and streams are part of a whole ecosystem. It's not just a problem of polluting the water. When you channel rivers or cut down the trees along the banks or pave over creeks, you don't just destroy the life in the water. The rivers get muddy or dry up. You're really changing the landscape."

"Human beings have been changing the landscape for centuries," objected Aunt Ceci.

"Carpenters!" said Janie, but she smiled.

Willa wanted to tell Janie that she understood what she meant, especially after today. The water at the spring in the ravine ran clear as glass, but by the time it came to the construction site where trees had been chopped down, the water looked tired and muddy.

But instead she yawned, and Janie took her dish towel out of her hands. "It's late. You're tired. Did you and Tabby have fun today?"

All Willa could do was nod.

Aunt Ceci came upstairs after Willa had gotten into bed.

"Look what I found," she said, "a letter to you. It got stuck inside my copy of the *Journal of Light Construction* that was delivered today!"

Aunt Ceci looked at Willa, expecting to see excitement or pleasure, but all Willa said was, "Oh, thanks. It's from Emma."

"A friend of yours?"

"Yeah . . .well, not so much anymore. She used to be my best friend, until around Christmastime."

"Did you have a fight?"

"No, not really. It was just . . . this other girl decided she wanted to be friends with Emma. Emma said we could all be friends, but . . ."

"I see." Aunt Ceci studied the letter, which Willa held tightly, unopened. "Did you try that?"

"No way!"

"Don't you like this other girl?"

"She took my friend away, how could I like her?"

"But other than that . . . is she a terrible person?"

"No . . . ," Willa said reluctantly. "It's just that—she's one of those perfect girls. I can't explain it. She's smart, she's pretty, she writes poetry."

"So in other circumstances, she might not be such a bad person to know."

Willa was silent. She remembered how, when Parker was just getting to know Emma, that Emma always invited Willa to join them. It was Willa who said no, after a few times. She'd wanted to make Emma choose. She'd forced Emma to choose.

Aunt Ceci didn't say anything more except good night. She gave Willa a hug and went downstairs again.

Willa reluctantly opened the envelope. She expected the letter to be full of stories about what a great time Emma and Parker were having at camp, stories that would just make Willa feel more jealous and left out.

But instead there was news of a different kind. Parker had left camp and gone back to Chicago. Her mother and father were getting a divorce, and her mother said she needed Parker with her.

Emma wrote, "Parker feels terrible. She knows your parents are divorced. Maybe—could you call her or e-mail her sometime, Willa?"

Call Parker? E-mail Parker! Emma had enclosed Parker's phone number and e-mail address. But what could Willa tell Parker except that when the two people you love most in the world don't get along, it hurts.

And Parker probably already knew that.

Willa lay in bed watching the moon out the window. The more she thought about divorce, the more she felt sorry for Parker, in spite of herself. She wanted to say something nice to her, to tell her that time would pass and that she'd get used to living with her mother and only seeing her father sometimes.

Willa lay there in bed thinking about Papa and Cindi and the new baby, and Ed visiting them without her, and she got sadder and sadder.

Then the memory of the cool, clear bubbling spring came to her. It was a miracle that it came out of the earth like that.

A clear spring. No one's property but the earth's.

Chapter 13

The next day was Saturday. It was gray and wet when Willa woke up. The rain slapped sadly at the flowers and dripped forlornly down the windows. Janie and Aunt Ceci both slept in late and Willa tried to be quiet. She drew a map in her field journal of the ravine and the spring, and described what she and Tabby had seen yesterday. It made her feel bad that she had to carefully tear the page out. She couldn't risk Janie seeing it before the report came back. *Then* she could brag about their adventure, but not yet.

How long would it be until they heard from the agency? It made Willa anxious to realize she couldn't send her water samples off until Monday morning.

The morning dragged after breakfast. While Aunt Ceci cleaned, Janie made phone calls. It kept raining.

Willa looked through their books and finally settled on one about organic gardening.

Around noon, the doorbell rang. It was Phyllis and Tran with Tabby. Phyllis had only recently gotten her driver's license and was very proud and very nervous that she'd made it all the way across the city, south to north. Tran and Phyllis were going to the movies, and they wanted to leave Tabby with Willa.

Why couldn't they go along, Tabby and Willa wanted to know.

"Because it's a film you wouldn't understand," said Phyllis.

"It's a serious film," Tran added. But she winked at Phyllis. Tran was tiny next to her friend. Her black hair stuck up in all directions and her clothes were trendy. She and Phyllis had been best friends "since forever," Tabby had said. "When the two of them get together it's like they're in their own private world."

Janie had a suggestion. "If you're going to a multiplex, then maybe Willa and Tabby could see something else."

Tran started to nod, but Phyllis burst out, "We don't *want* them to come with us. They're too *young*."

The two of them made a quick rush for the door, and Tabby and Willa went into a sulk. Willa was mortified. Did Phyllis really think she was such a baby?

When Willa had flown out to Seattle *by herself?* When Tabby and Willa had taken the bus yesterday to the high school and investigated the ravine?

It rained and rained. Janie suggested a jigsaw puzzle or Scrabble. Aunt Ceci said they could make birdhouses. At home Willa's mother would have just gotten a video for Willa, but Aunt Ceci and Janie didn't even have a TV. At first Willa had thought that was kind of cool, but not today.

Aunt Ceci said, "I don't suppose you'd like to look at some old photographs?"

She seemed surprised when Tabby and Willa said, "Yes!"

The photographs were in boxes upstairs in the storage room behind the red door. It was cozy up under the roof with the rain thrumming overhead. Willa and Tabby sat cross-legged on the wood floor, and Rain curled up in Willa's lap.

Aunt Ceci pulled out a tin box of black and white and brownish photographs. They showed some well-dressed women in white frilly dresses, some with parasols, standing in groups in front of a large house with a wide porch draped with flowering vines.

"This is my father's—your grandfather's—family. He had three aunts: Cecilia, Elena, and Teresa. His mother was the youngest sister; her name was

Amelia. She was the only one who married. They were a well-off family when the girls were growing up. Their father was a lawyer and a landowner in Colón in northern Panama.

"Here's a photograph of Amelia and Alberto when they got married." They were a young, good-looking pair. Amelia wore a straight, beaded dress with a train, and Alberto a tuxedo. He had a little mustache.

"According to family stories, your great-grandfather Alberto was a smooth talker who had big plans to buy up proerty in Colón. When the Depression came, the prices for property went down, and he lost a lot of money. He and Amelia had to move back to the family house, with all the sisters.

"That's how my father grew up, in a big house, in a well-respected but no longer rich family. He was the only child, and was he spoiled."

Aunt Ceci passed photographs of a handsome little boy who always seemed to be dressed in a suit. "Your grandfather, Fernando Lopez, grew up thinking he was the center of the universe," she said. "And he was, to all those doting aunts."

"Your Grandma Josie's life was very different." Aunt Ceci pulled out an album. It was white leather, a little cracked and worn at the corners, but the photographs inside were mostly in color, and they looked

American. There was a Chevrolet and a barbecue and cocker spaniel. There was a girl in a poodle skirt and a ponytail, wearing roller skates.

"Now this is an interesting story, how Josie and Fernando met," said Aunt Ceci, and Tabby and Willa leaned forward expectantly.

"My great-grandmother, my mother's grandmother Maria, was a maid to the Lopez family in their best days. She worked for the sisters until they couldn't afford her anymore, then she got married and had a daughter, Rosa. Rosa met an American called Tom Bright, who was stationed in Panama. When the war started he was sent to San Diego. He married Rosa so she could go with him. So your Grandma Josie was born in San Diego.

"She grew up in America, and you can see she was a typical American girl, except she spoke Spanish with her mother. She also heard all kinds of magical stories about Panama and especially about the rich and glamorous family in Colón that her grandmother had worked for.

"When Josie was eighteen, she and her mother went back to Panama for a visit. They walked by the Lopez house so that Rosa could show it to her daughter, and there was Fernando just coming out the door. He was about ten years older than her. He'd gone to college but never really settled at anything and still lived at home. But Josie didn't know that. She thought he was the handsomest man she'd ever seen. The next thing anybody knew, they were married. The Lopez family thought it was terrible that Fernando married the granddaughter of the maid, because that's how they still thought of Rosa's mother. So Fernando and Josie left very soon for San Diego and that's where they brought us up."

Now Aunt Ceci began to show photographs in another scrapbook. There was a bungalow surrounded by palm trees. Three little children with round cheeks and curly black hair splashed in a wading pool, with a beautiful woman behind them. She had frosted hair and was smoking.

Tabby said excitedly, "That's Grandma Josie. There's my mom. There's Willa's dad. And there's *you,* Aunt Ceci."

"Three little piglets," said Aunt Ceci. "And she had all the work of taking care of us. Papa came from a household where the man was king and didn't have to lift a finger. He was a big dreamer, like his own papa, and a natural salesman. He became a car salesman. The Latino community loved him. But he couldn't save a penny. Your grandma finally had it with him."

Willa had always been a little frightened of her Grandma Josie, who wore a lot of makeup and always had a new hairstyle or wig. She'd gone into the cosmetics business after she got divorced and had been very successful. She married again, and she and her new husband bought a ranch house and drove a Cadillac. Willa's mother and Grandma Josie had never gotten along. As for Grandpa Fernando, he'd gone back to Panama, and Willa couldn't remember him at all.

"Have you ever been to Panama, Aunt Ceci?" asked Tabby.

"No, none of us kids have ever been there," said Aunt Ceci. "I'd love to go someday. And of course Janie is wild to go to both Costa Rica and Panama to see the nature preserves."

Willa was still poring over the photographs of her father and his two sisters growing up. There was something she really wanted to know. Finally she asked, "Why is it that Tabby's mom and my dad don't get along?"

Tabby looked interested, too. This wasn't news to her, but the answer might be.

Aunt Ceci began to put the scrapbooks back in the boxes. "They had a big rivalry growing up. You know, there's only about a year between them. I'm three years younger, so I was the baby, but Carmen and Tommy were always fighting. They fought just like our parents did. Our parents had been very much in love, but they had too little money most of the time. My papa wasn't a bad guy, but he had a way of vanishing when things got tough. Then Mama got stuck with the rent and bills. She was angry—who wouldn't be—and that made Papa stay away more."

Aunt Ceci sighed. "Tommy took Papa's side and Carmen took Mama's, it's as simple as that. Over the years, even after Papa moved back to Panama, they just got more distant. It's sad, really. I love Tommy and Carmen a lot. I wish they'd make up."

Tabby thought about all this. "I want to speak Spanish," she said. "I want to go to Panama." She jumped up and began tap dancing. "Pan-a-ma!" she sang.

All Willa really knew about Panama was that there was a big canal there. She'd never heard these stories of the aunts before, or of little Fernando in his fancy suit, or of the romantic meeting between Fernando and Josie. Willa hardly spoke a word of Spanish. When she was little her father used to teach her phrases, but he didn't really speak it either, just like Aunt Ceci and Aunt Carmen didn't. It was funny, Willa thought, the way languages could be forgotten by a whole family. Sometimes people asked her why her name was Lopez since she didn't look Latina. Willa's hair was brown and straight, and her eyes were blue like her mother's.

Tabby didn't look Latina either. She looked African American. But the two of them were partly Latina. Half!

"I want to go to Panama, too," Willa said, jumping up and joining Tabby in her dance.

"*Vámonos a Panamá,*" said Aunt Ceci. "We'll all go together, someday soon, okay?"

"*¡Sí, sí, sí!*" said Tabby and Willa.

Chapter 14

On Monday morning Willa was eager to send her water samples to the Surface Water Management Program, but at first she wasn't sure how she was going to do it. Then Janie got a phone call. She was needed right away at Salmon Creek Park.

On Sunday night vandals had broken through the gate and someone in a big truck had driven around in a figure eight pattern on the lawn by the playground. They'd sprayed the restroom walls with graffiti and overturned the trash cans.

Janie looked grim as she drove off, promising to be back in an hour or two. Usually Willa wasn't left alone at the house, but after two weeks, Janie seemed to feel confident that Willa was okay there for short periods. Besides, it was an emergency.

As soon as she was gone, Willa labeled each of the vials and wrapped them carefully in some bubble wrap she found in the basement, and then packed everything with more bubble wrap inside a sturdy cardboard box.

She also enclosed a letter:

> Dear King Country Surface Water Management Program,
>
> Please test these two water samples. They come from a high school construction site. Sample A is from above the site. Sample B is from below the site. Please send the results to Janie Harmond at the Salmon Creek Environmental Center.
>
> Thank you,
> Willa C. Lopez

Hoping she was not being too dramatic, she added a p.s.

> This is top secret. The water may be poisoned.

Her mother said sometimes you had to exaggerate to get people's attention about a problem.

Willa felt proud of herself for having carried out this mission. When the report came back to Janie, how impressed she'd be that Willa had done this on her own.

The post office was only two blocks away, and there was a McDonald's a few blocks further. To celebrate, Willa had a Big Mac. She'd been missing McDonald's, but hadn't dared ask to eat there.

Tonight was a dress rehearsal of *Lady Windermere's Fan,* and they were all planning to go together from Uncle James and Aunt Carmen's house. Uncle James had started up the barbecue and the smell of mesquite charcoal filled the backyard. Aunt Carmen had already gone to the theater to put on her makeup and dress. She said she was too nervous to eat anyway.

Tabby was going to meet them at the theater, too. A friend's father would drop her off after her tap dancing class. Phyllis was out in the driveway, shooting hoops.

Willa heard Janie talking to Uncle James. "At a conservative estimate, the people who did this caused about five thousand dollars' worth of damage. That's a big chunk of our budget for grounds maintenance."

"I don't understand destruction like that," said Uncle James. "I see it all the time driving around the city. I know it's supposed to come from boredom or anger, but I just don't get it—especially in a beautiful park like that. Does it really make whoever did it feel powerful?"

"One of the worse things they did was pour motor oil in the creek. I can't believe anyone would do that," said Janie. "The rest of it, driving around on the grass and dumping trash cans, could just have been extremely misguided high spirits. But polluting the salmon stream is malicious. The oil was all over the rocks. Why?"

Uncle James just shook his head. "I don't know what the world is coming to, sometimes."

Willa wandered away from the adults. It always made her nervous when adults started going on about what the world was coming to. Papa could get into that kind of talk very easily—how when *he* was a kid, oh sure, they did a few bad things, *innocent* bad things. *Nowadays* there was a lot more destructiveness. It was all this TV violence and these computer games.

Willa would feel guilty and kind of mad, too. It wasn't her fault. They'd made this world that she was born into. They made the computer games and they made the TV shows. They were adults. They were born first.

She joined Phyllis in the driveway. "Can I shoot?" she asked.

"Sure," said Phyllis, tall as a skyscraper and with legs like steel. "Here."

Willa almost missed the ball, and tried to turn her awkward fumble into a dribble. Then she threw the ball, one handed, in the direction of the hoop. She meant it to look casual. It missed the hoop by a mile.

"Whoa, you taught you to shoot?" Phyllis laughed. But it didn't sound sarcastic. She came over to Willa and stood behind her. Phyllis put her arms around Willa's arms and showed her how to place her hands on the ball.

"Before you try the fancy one-handed shots, you need to practice the basics over and over until you get it right."

Phyllis took the ball back and modeled how she stood and how she bent her knees and how she gave a big spring upward as she shot. "It's not just your hands or your arms," she said. "You've got to put your legs into it, and your back. Use your whole body from your heels to your fingertips."

She demonstrated, crouching and pushing upward so that her strong calves tensed and her thighs contracted, and her back under the sweaty T-shirt was smooth with muscles. The energy moved right up through Phyllis's legs, back, and arms and into the orange ball. Then the ball left her hands in a perfect arc toward the circle of the hoop.

"This is how you do it when you don't have a bunch of tall, vicious girls coming at you every which way," Phyllis smiled. "Which is just about never the case." She tossed the ball to Willa. "Now you try it—and think about your feet."

After a half hour of this, Willa was sweaty, but happy. She'd had lessons from one of the best: a high school basketball star. They broke off to eat salmon and tabouleh salad and French bread, and then Phyllis and Willa went upstairs to take showers and change clothes.

She went into Phyllis's room for the first time. The walls were covered with posters of the University of Washington Huskies, the women's basketball team. There were also dozens of black and white photographs of girls playing basketball, as well as of lakes and skies and urban scenes. Willa knew that Phyllis had taken them all. Phyllis was so talented. She seemed to have the world at her feet.

"So, are you going to be a photographer?" Willa asked.

"Yeah, maybe," Phyllis said. "Or maybe I'll make movies. I want to get a video camera, but my dad says

I have earn the money for it myself. He suggested I try to sell my photographs, so I'm just learning to do that. It's kind of scary to think about people paying money for what I do."

"Why?" asked Willa.

Phyllis turned from the mirror where she'd been trying to do something with her hair.

"Well, it's like selling yourself. You're being judged. You don't look at what you did from the inside any-more, how you felt when you were doing it. You look at it from the outside, though the eyes of the person who's buying it. Who you *want* to buy it. And that's scary, because what if worrying about selling your vision makes you try to change it?"

Willa pondered this. "There are so many kinds of work," she finally said. "I used to think that most people worked in offices or factories or stores, but everybody I've met out here seems like they're doing something active or outdoors or artistic. I didn't know you could get paid to do things that are fun."

Phyllis laughed, even as she looked critically at herself in the mirror. Something about how she looked didn't please her, but Willa couldn't see what it was. She thought Phyllis was beautiful. Maybe it had something to do with boys.

"Well," Phyllis said, "if we had to depend on my

mom's salary, I can tell you we wouldn't be eating salmon for dinner. In school we hear about the bad old days when women couldn't work and stayed home and raised the kids. Now we can do everything, but what happens when the work you love doesn't pay?"

"What if," said Willa, "the man is the artist and the wife has a good job and supports him?"

"No way am I supporting some guy," Phyllis said. "Not even Anthony."

"The worst would be if you were *both* artists."

"The worst—or the best," said Phyllis. "You'd have a lot in common."

"You'll make money as a photographer," Willa predicted. "Maybe you could be a sports photographer."

"You think so?" Phyllis cheered up. She turned her back on the mirror and raced out of the bedroom and down the stairs, with Willa following.

Chapter 15

Even though Aunt Carmen had told them that dress rehearsals were almost always disasters, and that the only time to be worried was when the dress rehearsal went *well,* Willa was still surprised at just how bad that evening's performance was.

Actors forgot lines and had to be reminded. The English accents came and went. Some of the best lines, like "Because I think that life is too important a thing ever to talk seriously about," didn't sound funny anymore. The spotlight flickered onto the wrong faces at the wrong times, and some other scenes were lit as if underwater. Someone opening a door dramatically had the knob come off in his hand. A lady choked on her tea and had to be pounded on the back.

The director, Pete, was deathly calm at times, groaning loudly at others. The dress rehearsal was supposed to be like a real performance, so he couldn't interrupt to scream at the actors. He was only supposed to be taking notes to give them later, Aunt Carmen had explained. But during one scene, Pete was heard to say to himself and everyone around him, "Is this *Gone With the Wind?* Is this *Gone With the Wind?* Why are these women acting like Southern belles at a picnic?"

The best thing was that everybody was in costume and the costumes were very grand. Aunt Carmen looked completely different in a gray wig underneath a hat the size of a small chair, and in a dress with a sweeping train. Privately Willa thought that she was the best of the actors. But Aunt Carmen was only on stage a lot in the first act.

Aunt Ceci and Janie took Willa home before the play was completely over.

"They'll be up half the night," predicted Aunt Ceci.

"'We are all in the gutter, but some of us are looking at the stars,'" Janie quoted from the play, and they both began to laugh hysterically.

But Willa thought it was a beautiful thing to say, and resolved to remember it for the right occasion.

She looked at the stars when she got into bed that night, and wished Ed had been here to see the play too. She'd talked to him on the weekend; he said he was having a great time in San Diego. He had a tennis buddy and he went to the beach all the time. "I love it out here," he said, "I wish I could live here all year round."

Willa worried about that. What if Ed decided he wanted to stay with Papa? She knew her mother and father only pretended to get along, and that her mother had never really forgiven him. She knew Papa used to be late with his child support payments, and that was why they'd gone to Chicago, to live for a while with Aunt Stephie, her mother's sister. That was why her mother had gotten the job at American Gypsum. Willa knew her mom believed she'd had all the work of raising the two of them. If Ed chose Papa, her mom would feel awful.

All the same, Willa could understand wanting to live somewhere other than Chicago and wanting a different life. She resolved never to take sides against her brother over their parents, the way Papa and Aunt Carmen had done. She would never even fight with him again, never—even if he called her "Chip" because of her round cheeks. But he hadn't done that for a long time, now that he was older. Willa missed him terribly, but somehow she felt closer to him, now that they were both out of the house and living in different cities. She lay there thinking about how odd that was, while she looked at the stars.

The next day Janie took Willa with her to Salmon Creek Park. Some of the damage caused by the vandals was fixed already. The picnic tables and trash cans were turned upright again, and volunteers were already painting over the graffiti on the rest room walls. But the tire tracks all over the grassy lawn still remained, a terrible reminder of somebody's wild ride.

"The problem is that the police department is already stretched to the limit," the senior naturalist, Greg, was saying on the phone as they came into the office upstairs. Greg had white hair, but his eyebrows here still black. When he hung up, he shook his head. "That was one of the park's neighbors. She wants us to hire a private security guard to protect the park at night. I was too polite to say, 'With what funding, ma'am?'"

"At least we've got the trash and oil out of the creek. Fortunately it didn't seriously damage the restoration," Deb, another staff member said. "That's a relief, after all the volunteer work that's been done there."

They all started talking about the vandalism again, and Willa wandered downstairs. She looked, as she had a dozen times, at the exhibits Janie had created. Each one told a different story: the salmon life cycle; beachcombing; wetlands; birds at Salmon Creek Park. Next to each display made of poster board, construction paper, and photographs was a box full of various objects. When school groups came through, Janie or another nature teacher would take things out of the box and talk about them.

In the box about birds were feathers, eggshells, a fallen nest carefully preserved in a Ziploc bag, and lots of pictures. In the box about beachcombing were stones and shells, small chunks of driftwood, seagull feathers, and seaweed. Willa sniffed her hands after she put everything in this box away. She could smell the sea.

What an interesting park this is, thought Willa, going to the doorway and breathing deeply. The sweet scent of cedar and fir trees floated in the warm air. Down by the creek, Willa remembered, the air smelled fresh and a little muddy, while in the wetland it smelled of reeds and decayed leaves and soggy fallen branches. Behind all these damp and earthy smells was the salty sting of the ocean and the shore.

She wished she could figure out a way to draw a picture of the whole thing at once. In her field journal she had small sketches and some descriptions of what she had noticed. She even had some maps. In her private diary she wrote descriptions of what she did everyday and sometimes how she felt. The two journals, the two ways of seeing, didn't go together yet. She would almost need a third journal, one that was more like a treasure chest, where she could put everything she was coming to know about this particular place and how she felt when she was here.

Willa stood in the doorway, feeling her lungs swell with air that was complex and delicious. Then a truck came blasting up the road. Its windows were open and the radio was on and it was going way too fast. For an instant everything around Willa vanished—no more bird song, no more trees rustling in the warm wind, no more rush of water over in the creek—just car exhaust and electronic shrieking.

Willa caught a glimpse of the driver—a skinny young man with a slash of dark eyebrows in a pale face—and of his license plate: ROADIE 789.

Road hog is more like it, Willa thought, and suddenly was very angry.

She set off down the road in search of him.

There were two other cars parked next to ROADIE 789 in the lot by the wetlands. All of them had on the same radio station—not very loud, but loud enough to make a rumbling echo. One of the young men, wider around the middle than at the shoulders, and with floppy blond hair, was talking into a cell phone. The other man was thin, with a stubbly chin. He was polishing his car.

Drug dealers, thought Willa, creeping a little closer through the bushes. She heard the words, "I'll be home soon, Mom. I can help Dad with the mowing."

Mom and *Dad* were obviously code words, Willa decided.

ROADIE 789 got out of his truck. With deliberate, sinister strides, he approached the thicket where Willa was hiding. His jaw was heavy, and his eyes were dark windows in his pale face. What would he do to Willa when he saw her? She held her breath.

He gave a really big yawn, then a kind of rough laugh. He said, to no one in particular, "These all-nighters are killing me," and turned back to the others.

Twigs crackled around Willa as she stepped back in relief.

"What was that?" said ROADIE 789, but Willa had already back out of the thicket.

She was on the path leading back to the road when

Janie caught up with her. Janie was wearing her green Seattle Parks Service jacket.

"Willa! There you are."

Janie didn't come right out and say it, but she had been worried, Willa realized.

Willa blurted out, "I was wondering if those guys who hang out in the parking lot had anything to do with the vandalism."

"Why? Did you hear them say anything?"

"No," Willa admitted. The *Mom* and *Dad* conversation wouldn't really sound suspicious if she repeated it.

"Well, I can go talk to them at least," said Janie.

When Janie and Willa came up, the blond guy and his thin friend were both polishing their cars, and ROADIE 789 had the hood of his truck up and peering deep inside.

"Yes, ma'am?" he said when he saw Janie in her official jacket. "Anything I can do to help you?"

Janie was pleasant but firm. "We had some vandalism in the park the night before last. We're wondering if you saw or heard anything?"

"Not me, ma'am. I work late every night as a stagehand. When I'm done, I'm ready to sleep."

"What about you two?" Janie asked the others.

Willa thought the blond guy with the cell phone

in his pocket looked a little nervous. He said, "What did they do?"

"Dumped oil in the creek, overturned the trash cans. There was graffitti in the washrooms and tire tracks in circles on the grass in the upper park."

ROADIE 789 said smoothly, "Now, that's a shame. No, my friends and I haven't heard about it."

Jane nodded politely and thanked them. She and Willa went back down the path.

Willa thought it was strange that ROADIE 789 seemed to speak for all of them. Maybe *he* hadn't heard about it, but why did he think *they* hadn't?

"You should check the tire tracks, Janie," suggested Willa. "Compare the ones in the grass with the ones these guys have made."

Janie considered this, then said, "I've seen these guys around. They're probably pretty harmless. Anyway, if they did something Sunday night, why would they return to the scene of the crime so soon? It's fine to play detective, Willa, but let's not let our imaginations run away with things, okay?"

"Okay," said Willa reluctantly.

But Janie was quiet on the way back to the nature center.

Chapter 16

A few days later, when Janie and Willa got home from an afternoon errand, they found Aunt Ceci out in the backyard reading the paper. She didn't look up with a smile as she usually did and ask them what they'd been up to.

"A guy from the Surface Water Management Program was out at the site today," she said. "Taking samples from the stream. I heard through the grapevine that there had been a complaint. Everybody thought it was the neighbors, no big deal. But when I got home today there was a phone message from someone at this agency. Apparently Salmon Creek Park gave the guy your home phone number, Janie."

Janie looked puzzled, "We did send them a sample from the creek after the vandalism, but why would they call me at home instead of talking to Greg or Deb?"

"It wasn't about Salmon Creek," said Aunt Ceci, looking hard at her niece. "They wanted to talk to Willa about the water samples she sent them. They said they hadn't found anything to show that the stream by the high school was polluted, but they would investigate further, especially since you said the stream was 'poisoned.' They wanted to know if you had witnessed any dumping." Aunt Ceci paused. "I saved the message if you want to hear it, Willa."

Willa was too stunned to speak. She'd imagined it all differently. She thought the stream would be polluted and the agency would call Janie. Janie would realize how courageous and smart Willa was, and everybody would be grateful to her. What had made her imagine all that? What had made her write POISONED in her letter?

"What I want to know," said Aunt Ceci sternly, "is how you managed to take the samples from the stream. I know you didn't do it the day you visited."

So the story had to come out, about asking Aunt Carmen to drop Willa and Tabby at the mall and then taking a bus to the site and hiking up the ravine.

"Honestly, it was perfectly safe," said Willa, leaving out the part about the man with the barking dog.

"The bottom line," said Aunt Ceci, "is that you told Carmen a lie about where you were going. She never would have let you and Tabby take a bus off by yourselves. Tabby is even younger than you are. And anyway, I told you the stream was fine. No one was dumping anything!"

Janie asked, in a quieter voice, "When did you mail the samples?"

Willa told her. But she didn't tell her about McDonald's.

"I know your *intentions* were good, Willa," said Janie, and then looked at Aunt Ceci.

Willa nodded. She snuck a hopeful glance at Aunt Ceci. But her aunt's usually cheerful face was still stern. She suddenly reminded Willa a little of Grandma Josie.

"Just because it turned out all right this time doesn't mean it's all right, what you did. I don't want you thinking you can get away with stuff like this," she said. "I guess we'll have to tell Carmen."

"Not right away," said Janie quickly. "It's opening night tonight."

"That's right," said Aunt Ceci, brightening, then looking worried. "I hope for everybody's sake it goes better than the dress rehearsal."

It went better than better. *Lady Windermere's Fan* went splendidly. As if by magic, the rough spots were ironed out, the dialogue bounced back and forth. Although the actors were pretending to be in a drawing room with four walls, they weren't talking only to each other, but to the audience. Something in their bodies, and in their voices, thrived in the attention of the people outside that invisible fourth wall. The actors couldn't *show* that they liked the laughter—at least not by stopping everything and bowing—but they showed it by becoming more sparkling and dramatic. More *real.* It was as if they were just thinking up those witty lines on the spot.

There was a standing ovation that went on forever. The women in the cast and some of the men got bouquets of flowers. Willa and Tabby clapped until their hands felt like they'd fall off. They agreed that, of everybody in the play, Aunt Carmen was the best.

Afterward there was a cast party at Pete's house. It was an amazing place because Pete, in addition to being a play director, was an interior designer. The walls were red and the drapes were gold. Pete collected hats—maybe because he was bald—and they were arranged on hat racks around the house. There was a collection of straw hats in a pattern along one wall.

The cast kept their makeup on. Some of them still wore their costumes, and others had changed into street clothes. Aunt Carmen had gone from her brocade dress with the cinched-in waist to a velvet tunic—"I wouldn't be able to enjoy the chocolate cake with that corset on!"—but she was still wearing her sweeping hat.

When all the adults were safely occupied in conversation, Willa gestured Tabby and Phyllis into a quiet hallway and told them what had happened.

Tabby was worried. "Do you think they'll really tell my mom?"

"Maybe not," said Willa. "Anyway, we can just say it was my idea and my fault."

Phyllis was looking at Willa with new respect. "I'm not saying it was a good thing to do," she said, "but it shows some guts. You had the right idea, and maybe after they think about it, they'll be glad you proved the stream isn't polluted."

Polluted streams made Willa remember ROADIE 789. She told Phyllis and Tabby, "I think he and his friends are probably the ones who did the damage to Salmon Creek Park. It wouldn't take much work to prove it."

"Nature cop, that's what you are," said Phyllis, laughing. "Eco-detective."

"Really," insisted Willa, "all you'd have to do is measure the tire tracks on the playground and then his truck tires. I told Janie, but I don't think she's going to do any measuring."

"If I took pictures," said Phyllis thoughtfully, "I could blow up prints of the two sets of tire tracks. I have a friend with a darkroom. Then we could compare the tracks."

"We should do it soon," said Willa. "Before the grass grows back on the playground."

"We could go this weekend and tell everybody we're . . ."

"Going to the mall?" Willa shook her head. "I don't want to say I'm going somewhere when I'm not."

"Don't you go to Salmon Creek Park a lot with Janie while she's working?" asked Phyllis. "We could meet you there on Monday sometime. I can get the car."

"How will you take pictures if the truck is there?" Willa thought to ask.

"A telescopic lens. I can borrow a good one from my friend who has the darkroom. We'll have to get as close as we can without being noticed."

"We'll creep soundlessly through the jungle," Tabby said.

"You and Willa—soundless?" laughed Phyllis.

"What are you three giggling about?" asked Janie, coming up to them with a plate of cookies.

"Yum—cookies!" said Tabby, and they all took one and kept laughing.

Chapter 17

That weekend Janie went away to Victoria, Canada, for a conference on something called integrated pest management. That was a complicated way of talking about the good bugs, or "beneficials," who ate the bad bugs who ate the crops. If you used good bugs, Janie had explained, you didn't need to use chemical pesticides on the plants.

It didn't sound like a very interesting way to spend a glorious summer weekend, Willa thought, but then, grown-ups sometimes had strange ideas about what was fun.

Everybody else took full advantage of the warm weather. Uncle James went golfing with his buddies. Phyllis and Tran went on a killer-long bike ride on Vashon Island in Puget Sound. Aunt Ceci and Aunt

Carmen took Tabby and Willa swimming, and while Aunt Carmen dozed and polished her nails on a lounge chair by the side of the pool, Aunt Ceci joined the girls on the big slide. Although it was a little embarrassing that Aunt Ceci didn't shave her legs, she was clearly someone who knew what the good things in life were, just as much as her nieces. She enjoyed flying over the water and landing with a big splat.

Saturday night Uncle James took Aunt Carmen to the theater for the evening performance. Phyllis and Tran and their boyfriends were going, too. Aunt Ceci got a pizza—vegetarian on account of Tabby, but it was still good—and they sat outside at Tabby's house until late. Aunt Ceci seemed to have forgotten all about being mad at Willa the other day. The three of them laughed and made wild plans: they would go to Panama by ship; they would live in the rainforest and count butterflies; Aunt Ceci would show them how to build a tree house with a rope ladder.

Willa tried to think what she'd be doing if she was at home in Chicago. Ed would probably be at the computer and her mom would have her nose in a book and be encouraging Willa to do the same. Or else the three of them might be watching a video. Sometimes they took walks in their neighborhood on hot summer nights; Mom would buy them ice cream cones. Maybe, since it was the weekend, Willa would be at Emma's.

Emma! Willa stared up at the starry sky and realized she hadn't thought of her friend for several days. She had a sudden urge to write to Emma, not just a postcard, but a real letter, or an e-mail, to say, I'm having a wonderful time here. And—I miss you.

Willa spent Saturday night at Tabby's, and the next morning she followed her cousin out into the backyard. They sat for a while listening to the birds and watching the sky turn from pale pink and cream to bright blue. Willa couldn't believe that Tabby wanted to get up so early and work in the garden, but Tabby said early mornings were the best time. They pulled weeds and watered and tied some young pole beans more firmly to their trellises. Tabby had planted six different kinds of beans this year; Janie had given her the seeds and said they were heritage seeds. Some had been carried across America by the pioneers. Willa hadn't realized there could be so many kinds of beans. The only ones she knew were green beans, and she didn't like them much.

"Those string beans you get in the store are all the same," Tabby told her. "'Course they don't taste that good. They're grown on big industrial farms, Janie says."

The beans that Tabby grew weren't even all green; in another two or three weeks there would be red-striped pods and purple pods and yellow pods, she said, and when the pods dried there would be little dry beans inside. Willa had seen the glass jars of beans in Aunt Carmen's kitchen.

Tabby and Willa spent a long, quiet couple of hours in the garden before everybody got up and Uncle James decided to make waffles. Then they went swimming again, this time with Phyllis and Tran. And finally they went to the matinee performance of *Lady Windermere's Fan.*

When Willa got back to Aunt Ceci's there was a message for her from her mother, and Willa called her back.

To Willa's surprise, a man answered the phone. He sounded friendly when he heard it was Willa. Too friendly, Willa thought.

"Who was that?" she asked her mother. She had been next door at their neighbor's for a minute, which is why she hadn't picked up the phone.

"Oh, just a friend from my new book club who came over for dinner," her mother said. She went on to talk about the plans she was making to fly out to

Seattle later in the summer. "How about a vacation, just the two of us?" she asked. "We could rent a car and drive down the coast and see your dad and Cindi. And you, me, and Ed could fly home together."

"Okay," said Willa. She was worried. Usually when her mother mentioned Cindi, she sounded irritable, especially since Cindi had the baby.

Her mother kept chattering about this and that. Willa kept quiet and answered yes and no. She didn't say anything about beneficial insects or about beans, or even about *Lady Windermere's Fan*. She felt like she was back with her mother in their living room, not in Seattle. Everything was familiar except for one person, who was probably just sitting there, also listening to her mother.

Her mother never asked people over to dinner, Willa thought. She went out to lunch with women from work or to the movies with her old friend Sally sometimes. She used to have Aunt Stephie over a lot, with Aunt Stephie's different boyfriends, but Aunt Stephie had finally gotten married and gone to live in Akron.

No man had ever come to dinner on a Sunday night by himself.

No man had ever picked up their phone and answered when Willa called.

Chapter 18

Willa was restless that night and dreamed of rivers that rose up and swept trees downstream, and of ducks that swirled around in storms like toys. She woke up in the middle of the night and heard the front door opening. It took a moment to remember it was probably Janie, returning late from her conference in Canada. But not until Willa heard Janie and Aunt Ceci's voices whispering was she completely sure.

She lay awake for a while thinking about what she and Phyllis and Tabby planned to do in the morning; she *couldn't* forget to bring the tape measure. Then she was back to stormy dreams of rivers pouring into the sea. Once she thought she saw her mother sail by in a boat with a man who wasn't her father. She heard her mother's voice calling to her, sounding happy. "It's a watershed, Willa," she said.

When she woke, she'd kicked off all the covers. Rain the cat, who often slept at Willa's feet, had given up and gone to curl up on top of Willa's clothes on the chair.

Willa heard Aunt Ceci's truck drive off. That meant it was about six and her aunt was off to have her usual breakfast with the other women on the job. In addition to a laborer and another carpenter, there were now two women electricians working at the high school building site.

Willa couldn't get back to sleep. She had about an hour and a half to herself before Janie would get up. Her mind was racing in anticipation of the day ahead. She could go out to Aunt Ceci's workshop and get the tape measure. She could do some sit-ups and push-ups, which was what Phyllis did in the morning. She could wander out into the garden and pick slugs off the lettuce, which was what Tabby did in the morning. She could go into Janie's office and use her computer to write a letter to her mom or dad or Emma.

Thinking of her mother, Willa remembered her dream, and the man who answered the phone last night. What if her mother didn't want her back in

Chicago? What if her mother was getting married again? Willa remembered how hard it was when Papa got married again. Willa and Ed had gone to the wedding in San Diego. Strange people kept coming up to them and saying, "Welcome to the family." Cindi had three brothers and a sister, and about a million aunts and uncles. Sometimes Willa had overheard a whisper, "Those are the kids from the first marriage."

Papa was the kind of guy who didn't write a letter or call very often, but ever since Willa had come to Seattle, he'd been sending her e-mail, mostly jokes, and always signing them, "your loving Papa."

Willa tugged on a pair of shorts and a T-shirt and went next door to Janie's office. She thought of a line from *Lady Windermere's Fan*: "I can resist everything except temptation." Janie always let her use the computer, but Willa always asked first. Willa turned it on and checked her e-mail. There was a joke from Papa, but it wasn't that funny. Nothing from her mother. Willa knew she could write to Emma, but she was too restless somehow.

Instead, she looked at the things Janie had arranged on the shelves. In between the nests and bird skeletons and bottles and boxes was a framed photograph of two kids in an orchard. One of them was Janie when she was about Willa's age, and the other was her brother, who now owned the farm where they'd grown up in Oregon. Janie said they'd raised all their own food and sold pears and blueberries. They'd had bees, too, and in the summer Janie used to sell honey at a roadside stand.

No wonder Janie was a nature teacher, having grown up on a farm. Could you be a nature teacher, Willa wondered, if you'd grown up in a San Diego suburb or a Chicago apartment building? Could you be a nature teacher if, like Willa, you hardly knew the names of anything on earth? Was it too late to learn all that stuff now that she was twelve?

Willa flipped through one of Janie's field journals from years ago. In her neat handwriting she described watching spiders spin their webs in a corner of the kitchen. The pencil drawing was a little faded, but still clear. Janie had started her field journals when she was in high school, she'd told Willa. Janie had read a book called *Silent Spring* by Rachel Carson, about how pesticides were getting into the food chain and killing insects, birds, and animals. Because of Carson's book, a terrible pesticide called DDT had been outlawed. Carson was an activist, but she also wrote books because she loved nature so much. After *Silent Spring* Janie had gone on to read

Carson's two books about the sea, and many other books by nature writers, and she had decided to become a naturalist.

"You can't get a college degree in nature," Janie had told Willa. "You can do biology, botany, zoology, environmental science. But becoming a naturalist—well, it's almost an old-fashioned term. It makes you imagine a nineteenth-century writer like Henry Thoreau walking around Walden Pond looking at the way ice melts and describing it in his journals. In the old days, everybody made observations of the physical world. Now, only specialists do. But I still love that word—*naturalist.* I like it better than entomologist, which is what I once thought I'd be, when I was getting my undergraduate degree. Entomology is the study of insects. I thought I'd get a Ph.D. in bugs! I ended up more interested in education and went on to get a teacher's degree in environmental education."

Willa paged through more of Janie's field journals. Here was a drawing of clouds, here was one of bird tracks on the sand, all the things that Janie had noticed and thought interesting and tried to describe.

When her mother's friends in Chicago asked Willa what she was going to be when she grew up, they never said anything about nature. If she were to say biologist, they would think of her in a white coat in a laboratory. It was as if they didn't know there were jobs outdoors! But even in Chicago there were parks, and park rangers. You could work in a museum of natural history and go on expeditions and bring back plants and bones to study. Janie said the Field Museum in Chicago had wonderful collections, and Willa was lucky to live in a city where she could visit it all the time.

Willa went to her room and brought her own field journal back to the office. Compared to Janie's, it was pretty sloppy. Her handwriting wasn't that neat, and some of her drawings didn't look too much like what she had written the things were. But some pictures were cool—lichen on a branch and a speckled bit of bird egg. When she got home, she'd ask her mother to take her to the Field Museum.

Willa opened the journal to a fresh page and began to sketch one of the seagull feathers on the desk. First it looked good; then it started to look strange. It could have been a Christmas tree lying on its side. She remembered Janie had said Tabby had a gift for scientific illustration. When Tabby drew a leaf, you could tell what kind of tree it came from. When Tabby drew a feather, you could tell it was a feather!

It was almost seven. It occurred to Willa that what

she really wanted was to look at water under the microscope again. She'd never used Janie's microscope on her own, but it couldn't be that complicated, she thought. She still had a vial of the clear spring water. She'd sent the samples away to be tested, but, because of trying to keep the secret, she hadn't looked at the water herself.

Tiptoeing, Willa went to get the vial from her hiding place and brought it back. She took out a fresh slide from the box and found the eyedropper and squeezed out a little drop of water onto the slide. She slipped the slide under the lens and put her eye to the eyepiece.

It was blurry and she fiddled with the knob. She felt again the wonder of the dark green ravine with sparkles of light on the stream. She remembered how clear the water was as it bubbled up from underground. She recalled that mysterious sense that the water was coming straight from the heart of the earth.

Willa had knelt on the chair to get a better view into the eyepiece, when suddenly the chair rolled out from under her. Trying to steady herself, she grabbed at the closest thing at hand. Unfortunately, it was the microscope.

With a huge crash, she and the microscope hit the floor. The chair overturned, the vial of water fell and smashed. There was glass and water everywhere. It sounded like the end of the world.

Faster than Willa would have thought possible, Janie was upstairs and crouching down beside her.

"Are you all right?" For a moment all Janie saw was Willa on the floor, but then the whole disaster struck her. She told Willa not to move and began to gather up the pieces of glass. Then she helped Willa to her feet and righted the chair. Finally she turned to the microscope, as if she was afraid to see what had happened to it.

Janie put it on the desk again. The microscope was a little battered, but nothing was broken, not even the reflecting mirror. Willa breathed a sigh of relief, but her stomach got all tight again when Janie said, "What were you doing?"

Janie was always so cheerful that her stern question made Willa feel awful. It wasn't that Janie had ever told her she couldn't come in the office, but to come in and make a mess . . .

"I just wanted . . . ," Willa began, and stopped.

She'd wanted to look at a drop of water. How stupid did that sound?

Chapter 19

Janie and Willa usually had breakfast together. Willa had gradually gotten used to oatmeal and soy milk instead of eggs and bacon or Pop Tarts and cereal. This morning they both had granola and Janie had an extra cup of coffee. She'd accepted Willa's apologies, but Willa still felt bad.

Janie changed the subject to a more cheerful topic. She told Willa about the conference she'd just been to. Farmers all over the United States and Canada were getting interested in how to use beneficial insects to control the bad pests that ate the crops. Ladybugs were a good insect and so were green lacewings. If you could get a lot of ladybugs and green lacewings for your farm, you were set!

In spite of being glad that Janie was no longer

thinking about what had happened upstairs, eventually Willa began to fidget. She'd agreed to meet Phyllis and Tabby at ten. It was getting close to nine now, and Janie was still in her bathrobe.

"Aren't you going to work today?" Willa asked.

"Not this morning. I have a dentist's appointment downtown. Do you want to come with me? I'm going to work afterward."

"I'd rather stay here and . . . read. I promise not to get into any trouble."

"That's fine. I'll swing by here after my appointment and pick you up, and we'll go to Salmon Creek. It might be twelve or twelve-thirty, if I do a couple of errands."

Janie finally left around nine-thirty. Willa rushed to the phone. Maybe Tabby and Phyllis hadn't left yet, and she could let them know she wouldn't be at the park with Janie until the afternoon. But Aunt Carmen sleepily answered on the sixth ring.

"No, *querida,* I think Phyllis took Tabby swimming or something like that. They should be back around noon or so, because I need to use the car to go to an audition this afternoon. Oh! I should be getting ready. I need to study my lines, do my hair . . . I'll tell the girls you called."

Willa waited at home until 10:45. And then she

couldn't stand it any longer. Hadn't Phyllis and Tabby realized that something had changed in the plans? Why hadn't they called her? Why didn't they come by? Why hadn't they asked Greg or Deb where Janie was? Then they would have found out she had a dentist's appointment.

Phyllis and Tabby didn't think that Willa had chickened out on them, did they?

They couldn't go ahead and take the photographs and do the sleuthing without her.

Could they?

It was this last thought that made Willa go searching in the basement for Aunt Ceci's bike. She'd been to Salmon Creek Park often enough. It was only a couple of miles away. She could get there in twenty minutes and find Phyllis and Tabby. They'd do what they needed to do, and get her home by 12:30.

Janie would never know.

Willa started biking north. But it wasn't long before she grew uncertain. Many streets in Seattle didn't have names; they were numbered. Willa knew she had to turn left at some point—but where: 97? 108? 113?

In spite of the growing heat, Willa felt a little chill of fear go through her. Nothing was looking familiar. She hadn't remembered going uphill for one thing. You never noticed hills riding in a car. Suddenly she was certain she'd gone too far north. She decided to turn left. Then things *really* began to look unfamiliar. She passed a Vietnamese noodle restaurant, a car wash, and a strip mall. She stopped at a busy intersection and bought a soft drink at a 7–Eleven. Standing in the parking lot, Willa looked longingly at the payphone. Maybe she could call her father or her brother. Ed was good at figuring out how to get out of trouble. But they were in California. Wasn't there anyone here who could help her if she was lost?

There was Aunt Carmen. *She* seemed like a person who understood about things going suddenly and drastically wrong. But she also had a temper. What if she got mad at me, Willa thought. What if she got mad at Phyllis and Tabby? Besides, Aunt Carmen didn't have the car. She couldn't come get Willa.

The sun was hot overhead. Willa finished her drink. It wasn't very pleasant at the busy intersection. Then she thought of Uncle James. He was always kind and relaxed. His job was just to drive around all day inspecting people's houses, so he could easily drive by the 7–Eleven. Before she could change her mind, Willa went to the phone booth and hunted up the number of City Light.

She managed to get through to his department, but of course he couldn't come to the phone. He was "out in the field," as the woman said.

Willa left a more detailed message than she'd meant to. It got more detailed because the woman at the office grew more concerned. *"Where are you?"* she asked more and more urgently.

"Never mind, I'm all right," said Willa, and finally got off the phone. She felt a little nervous that the woman might be able to trace her call and send a cop car to find her.

Did she want to be found? Or did she want to stay lost? To figure things out on her own?

Willa went back into the 7–Eleven.

"Do you have a map of Seattle?" she asked.

"Over there."

Willa spread it out on the counter and found where she was, and where Salmon Creek Park was. "I'm meeting my cousins," she said to the woman at the counter, who hadn't asked.

Now that she had an idea where she was going—west to Puget Sound—she felt more cheerful. Nobody had to come get her. She wasn't lost after all.

She would be there in ten minutes!

Chapter 20

It was well past noon when Willa finally arrived at Salmon Creek Park. She was hot, thirsty, and tired. She was mad at herself for not actually *buying* the map, but relying on her memory. It was one thing to decide to go west, but a lot of dead-end streets went west, too.

The worst part was that in spite of all this effort, she was bound to have missed Phyllis and Tabby, missed the eco-sleuthing adventure, and the chance to be a hero. She wouldn't be a hero now. She'd be in trouble for taking off without even leaving a note. She'd been in far worse trouble than for sending the water samples off or knocking over Janie's microscope.

Wearily, Willa got off the bike and stretched her legs. She thought of going into the nature center and telling Greg and Deb that she was here, so that if Janie called, she wouldn't be worried. But then Greg and Deb would make her sit there in the office, and it would be worse than sitting in a dentist's office. Willa began to wheel her bike alongside the road. She wondered if there was a place she could stash it for a while. From the picnic area at the top of the bluff came the sound of children laughing and playing. Well, she could always go up to the playground and take measurements of the tire tracks. At least she'd remembered to bring the tape measure.

It was a brilliant summer day, but it wasn't as hot as it had been all week, she thought. There was a breeze stirring up, and thin white scarves of clouds dancing in the blue sky above. Maybe she could just live here in the woods for a time. She could scavenge food from the trash cans. She could get her water from the drinking fountains. She could make herself a hut of branches, or even a tree house. She wouldn't finish school; nature would be her school. Willa pictured herself like Henry Thoreau, the nineteenth-century writer and naturalist, living happily in the woods.

The breeze picked up and Willa shivered a little. She hadn't thought to bring a sweater. For the last week all she'd worn were T-shirts and shorts. What would she do if it rained? What was winter like in the Northwest? Janie had told her that the Indians here used to make rain-shedding capes of woven cedar bark.

In the open space of the playground it was warmer, and Willa set to work. The tracks were still visible. Willa measured them and wrote down the measurements in her field journal. That made her feel better. She decided to go down to the parking lot by the wetland and, if the cars weren't there, to measure those tracks too. She walked along the creek and crossed the bridge over to the wetland, where she leaned her bike against a tree. The breeze was stronger here, and it carried the sound of radios.

Oh, the guys were there, ROADIE 789 and his two friends. Through the thick shrubs she could see their open hoods. She would never get close enough to measure the tire tracks.

Suddenly she noticed ROADIE 789 coming toward her. She was in the bushes on one side of the wetland and he was on the other. His mouth twisted down with a cigarette on one side and his dark eyes scowled. He was carrying a pan of something that looked black and greasy.

I hope he's not going to dump that in the grass, Willa thought. But it was worse than that. He came toward the edge of the marsh and very deliberately poured the pan of used motor oil into the water.

"You can't do that!" shouted Willa, surprised at how loud and firm her voice was. Her body was shaking.

The man started at her voice and peered until he could see her in the bushes. Then, satisfied that she was just a kid, he ignored her. He even wiped out the pan with paper towels and tossed them in the bushes.

"Don't you know oil kills the plants and fish in the water?" Willa shouted, stepping forward.

"Says who?" He looked at her again, and his look was both sly and surprised. For just a second Willa thought that he might really have no idea how oil could cover the surface of the water and suffocate everything. The insects would get stuck and the plants would die from lack of sunlight. He might not know, because a few weeks ago, Willa hadn't known either. Not that she would have gone around dumping motor oil in a wetland—that was just common sense.

Then he flicked his cigarette butt in the water and turned away, and Willa realized it wasn't that he didn't know. He didn't care.

"It's against the law," she said recklessly. "I'm going to report you right now."

Then he said something that Willa wished she hadn't heard. She looked for help to the other men standing around their cards, but they didn't seem to be paying attention. As ROADIE 789 swore, he started toward her across the squishy ground, but then seemed to think better of getting his shoes wet and went back to his truck.

Willa ran back to where she'd left the bike and jumped on and started peddling along the trail. She'd go back to the nature center and report him to Greg and Deb. But the trail seemed too slow; the bike wheels kept jamming and sticking in the ruts. She headed for the main road instead.

The sound of the truck came at her from behind, as if it were the hot breath of a dragon chasing Willa. He roared past her, too close, then braked, so she almost ran into his back bumper. Willa made a flying leap off the bike, just as the truck came crunching backward over the bike.

The truck stopped. Willa, hearing his door open, got shakily to her feet and staggered behind a tree. Then she heard another car come roaring to a stop. ROADIE 789 slammed his door shut and gunned the motor, and he was out of there.

Footsteps came running, but Willa still hid behind the tree.

"Willa, Willa, are you okay?"

It was Phyllis and Tabby.

"I saw what that guy did," said Phyllis, helping Willa up. "He practically ran over you, and he did run over your bike."

"Aunt Ceci's bike," Willa said shakily.

"Never mind about that." Phyllis dusted the leaves and dirt off Willa. "Nothing broken?"

"Just a little sore."

"Did you just get here?" asked Tabby. "We waited for you for hours."

Quickly, Willa told them about Janie's dentist's appointment and how Willa had to change plans and get here on the bike.

"I . . . got turned around a little," she admitted.

"We got lost, too," said Tabby matter-of-factly. "Phyllis doesn't know how to read a map and . . ."

"But I do know how to take photographs," Phyllis interrupted.

"You got pictures of the tire tracks!"

"I got more than that," said Phyllis. "I got evidence of a crime in progress."

Chapter 21

"We parked the car in the upper parking lot," said Phyllis, "so I could take photographs of the tire tracks. Then Tabby and I came down to the wetland and creek."

"We were exploring," added Tabby.

"We found a spot up above the guys, where we could hear some of what they were saying and where I could take some pictures with the telescopic lens. First the guy who almost hit you, Mr. ROADIE, and his friend were the only ones there, and then the younger kid with the long blond hair drove up."

"We could hear them, Willa," said Tabby. "They were in an argument."

"Yeah," said Phyllis. "The blond kid was saying that he didn't like what ROADIE had done. He called him

Robert. He said his parents had been really upset about the damage. I got the impression that he lives around here."

"The other guy, the skinny one, wasn't saying anything all this time," said Tabby, and then made a face. "Robert finally curses and says, Nobody's going to tell me what to do. I can do whatever I want to this park. And he grabs this pan of motor oil and goes to the marsh."

"That's when we heard *you,* Willa, shouting at him not to dump the oil," said Phyllis. "We hadn't seen you before that, but I located you with my telescopic lens. *And* I got some photographs of him dumping the motor oil."

Willa felt somehow relieved knowing that she hadn't been so alone with ROADIE 789. It was starting to catch up with her, how scary it had been to have him shouting at her and coming after her in his big truck. What if she hadn't jumped off the bike in time when he braked?

Willa squared her shoulders. "We need witnesses."

Phyllis and Tabby looked at her. "We saw everything," Phyllis protested. "Or don't you think they'll believe girls?"

"I mean witnesses to the park vandalism," said Willa. "We should talk to his friends."

"Those guys?" said Tabby. "They're creepy! We should just tell Janie."

But then they heard the sound of a car coming toward them. It was the blond man. He stopped and got out of the car.

"Are you all right?" he asked Willa.

"*Now* you ask," said Phyllis. "I notice you didn't exactly rush over to stop him from chasing Willa and trying to run her down."

"I called the police," he said, surprising them. "I thought I'd better do that first, so that they had a chance of catching him."

Now that Willa looked at him up close she saw that, in spite of his stubbly beard, he wasn't much older than Phyllis.

"Did you tell the police about the dumping just now?"

"And about the park vandalism," he said. "Look, my name's Dylan. I live with my parents just a few blocks away. I've been coming to this park since I was a little kid. I met this guy Robert a few months ago. He seemed okay. He's given me tickets to a lot of concerts. He works as a stagehand, and sometimes goes on the road with a local band."

"Is that why he has the license plate ROADIE?" asked Willa.

"Yes," said Dylan. "Anyway, he's okay—usually—except when he's been drinking. Then he gets kind of mean and crazy. I've seen him like that once or twice. I didn't actually *see* him vandalizing the park last week, but after you"—he gestured to Willa—"came by with the park ranger, and Robert said he didn't know anything about it, I asked him point blank, was that true. He said, he supposed he'd gotten a little rowdy with a couple of his stagehand buddies after the big arena concert."

There was the sound of a police siren in the distance. They all looked at each other.

"Well," said Willa with satisfaction, "I guess we've got our witness."

"Let's all go to the nature center and tell them what happened," said Phyllis. "You too, Dylan."

He got back in his car. Phyllis put Aunt Ceci's mangled bike in her back seat and Tabby and Willa squeezed into the front.

When they got near the nature center, they saw Janie and a police officer standing together beside a blue-and-white cruiser. Another car pulled up with Seattle City Light written on the door. Uncle James was in the driver's seat, with a furious-looking Aunt Carmen next to him.

"Oh no," said Phyllis, putting on the brakes and

pulling over to the side of the road and hunching down.

Willa did the same and Tabby followed. The three girls peered over the dashboard. Meanwhile Dylan continued into the parking lot, got out of his car and went over to the officer. Willa could see them all talking. The officer returned to his car to use the radio while Janie listened to him. Janie asked Dylan something, and he shook his head in confusion and pointed to the parked car with, apparently, nobody in it.

The girls heard footsteps, running footsteps.

"Oh great," muttered Phyllis, still with her head down. "I barely got my license, and now I'm going to lose it."

"Phyllis!" said Janie, and yanked open the car door. Tabby and Willa tumbled out from the other side. "Willa! I've been so worried." She brought them over to the police car, explaining, "He came here because he got a call about the vandalism, but I was just telling him we've been looking for you all day, and I was just about to report you missing."

"Phyllis North!" said Aunt Carmen. "*Who* told you that you could take the car up here for hours, and with your younger sister, too? What's been going on here? And now I've missed my audition, too."

"Hi, Mom," Phyllis said weakly, and then, "Hi, Dad!" more hopefully.

Uncle James had scooped Tabby up in his arms. "Honey, what are you and your big sister and cousin doing up here?"

"Catching vandals!" Tabby said.

The cop got out of his car again. He was a strong, compact Asian man with a calm, friendly face.

"Are you all right?" he asked Willa. "Safe and sound?"

"Yes," said Willa, and then she quickly told them all about the man who dumped the oil.

"Your friend here"—he pointed to Dylan—"called nine-one-one about twenty minutes ago. Another officer stopped the guy and has taken him to the local station until we find out what the story is. I've come here to talk with Dylan. Did the rest of you see anything?"

"We're all witnesses," said Phyllis. "And I have photographs, too."

"Willa told him to stop," said Tabby. "So he chased her and ran over the bike and almost Willa, too."

"Oh no, Willa!" said Janie, clutching her.

"What's your name, young lady?" asked the officer.

"Willa C. Lopez . . . sir."

"Well, Willa C. Lopez, maybe you can tell me exactly

what happened," said the officer. "Then we'll see what the truck driver has to say for himself. If he threatened and attacked you, then he's in even more trouble."

"Oh, he's in big trouble, all right," said Phyllis. "Because he didn't just dump the oil today and chase Willa, he was the one who wrecked the park last week."

"And I know somebody else who's in big trouble, too," Aunt Carmen said sternly, but she looked a little less angry. She stroked Phyllis's shoulder. "If your dad hadn't gotten a message from the office that Willa was wandering around lost on her bike, we wouldn't have called Janie and figured out you were all probably up at the park together."

"The important thing is that we caught him!" said Phyllis, and Tabby and Willa nodded vigorously.

But Janie said, "No, the important thing is that you're all safe."

And nobody could argue with that.

A police detective came to the house that evening. Willa had to tell the story again, how ROADIE 789 had dumped the motor oil and then had come after her. Phyllis and Tabby would also have to say what they'd seen and heard. The detective would talk to them next. It made Willa feel important to be a witness, but also scared. The detective seemed to believe her and to write down everything she said. But Willa pictured herself in a courtroom, on the stand, with lawyers circling like sharks around her, trying to destroy her story.

"Ms. Lopez," they would say, "how can you be sure it was motor oil he was dumping? Were you close enough to see? Maybe it was only molasses. Did you ever think of that?" ROADIE 789's lawyer would stare her down and say, "My client only put on the brakes a little quickly. How was he to know you would almost crash into his truck? Weren't you following too closely?"

After the detective had gone, Willa told Aunt Ceci and Janie about her fears. Aunt Ceci laughed and said she'd been watching too many TV shows, but Janie said it was unlikely there would be a trial. There wasn't a need for one. Not only were there witnesses to the motor oil dumping, but Phyllis had taken photographs. Dylan would make a statement to say Robert had vandalized the park and dumped stuff into the creek the week before. Besides, Robert's main problem now wasn't vandalism. It was that four people had seen him threaten Willa.

ROADIE 789 wouldn't be out on the road for a while.

But neither would Phyllis. Aunt Carmen and Uncle James had revoked her driving privileges for a month.

Chapter 22

"It's not every day that a person turns twelve," said Aunt Ceci, bringing out a cake glowing with a dozen candles and one to grow on.

Even though Willa had been thinking of herself as twelve for a long time now, August 14 was still an important date. Now other people would think of her as twelve, too.

Finally.

Everybody was in Aunt Ceci and Janie's backyard, and everybody included Willa's mother. She'd flown in the day before yesterday, and tomorrow the two of them would be in a rental car, heading down the West Coast to San Diego.

Willa could hardly wait: two whole weeks with just her mom. They'd eat in restaurants and stay in motels. In Oregon they'd visit the Sea Lion Caves and take a boat across Crater Lake. They'd ride the cable cars in San Francisco and go to Universal Studios in Los Angeles. They'd see Papa and Cindi and the new baby, and then they'd fly home with Ed.

Willa glanced at her mother. Laura Saunders seemed happier and more relaxed than Willa had seen her in a long time. She wore no makeup and her hair was longer. She was wearing jeans and a T-shirt, like everybody else at the table except Aunt Carmen.

Aunt Carmen never wore jeans. When she wasn't in her bathrobe, she was in "full regalia," as Uncle James liked to say. *Lady Windermere's Fan* was over and she had dropped her grand manner as the Duchess of Berwick. Now she was in the early stages of rehearsal for *Macbeth.* She was one of the witches who said, "Double, double, toil and trouble."

But now Aunt Carmen was laughing and joking, and a crumb of chocolate cake at the corner of her mouth made her look anything but witchy.

Willa began to open her presents. A scrapbook of hand-pressed flowers and a cloth bag of lavender for scenting drawers came from Tabby. Phyllis gave her a poster of the Washington Huskies. Willa's mother gave her clothes—her mother always gave her clothes! From Janie there was a book on wetlands with lots of pictures. And there was something from Emma, too: a novel and a letter that said she missed Willa and was looking forward to seeing her again soon. Over the past month she and Willa had been emailing once or twice a week, and that had felt great. Willa was no longer mad at Emma, but happy that she'd be seeing her soon. Willa even thought it might not be impossible to give Parker a call when she got back to Chicago and to see how she was doing with her parents' divorce.

The largest gift Willa left till last. It was from Aunt Ceci, and from the shape of it, it looked like it might be a basketball. To Willa's amazement, it turned out to be a microscope—a microscope of her own—with a kit for making slides.

Bursting with happiness, she threw her arms around Aunt Ceci. How she'd miss all of them! There'd be no more swims with Tabby or basketball practice with Phyllis, no more rehearsals with Aunt Carmen or making birdhouses with Aunt Ceci. There'd be no more walks with Janie or helping her put together exhibits on "Forest Ecology" and "What You Put in Your Storm Drain Comes Out in Salmon Creek."

Instead, Willa would be back in Chicago, going into the seventh grade. Life would settle back into its routine—school and friends, homework and reading, TV and computer games. Some things would be different: Willa had resolved to get on the basketball team. She'd try to interest Emma in birdwatching or urban ecology. She'd go to the Field Museum with a notebook, and think of Janie as she drew pictures of the exhibits. Janie had made her promise that they'd write and send each other sketches.

Some other things might be different, too. Willa's mother had said she was looking forward to introducing someone to Willa and Ed. Hugh, the man from the book club, was looking forward to meeting them, too.

Oh oh.

But as Ed had said when they'd talked about it on the phone, maybe he'd be a great guy. If Ed could give him a chance, so could Willa.

Yesterday, Willa had gone with her mother and Janie to Salmon Creek Park. It was a dry summer's day, with just a tang of autumn coming. No leaves had turned color of course—it was still mid-August—but there was something deliciously toasty about the scent of the maples and of the fir needles under their feet.

"This all feels really new to me," Willa's mother had kept saying. "I know I was here years ago, but I'd forgotten how big the trees are, and how *green* everything is. It smells divine."

Willa's mom had been surprised—and pleased—that Willa knew so much about everything at the park. Willa not only knew the names of many birds and insects, but she knew something about the ways things seemed to fit together: the watershed created habitat for birds and animals; the trees along the creek shaded the water so it wasn't too hot for the salmon, who returned to lay their eggs in the autumn.

"You're quite the naturalist," her mom kept saying.

It was Willa's secret—she hadn't even told Janie—that she planned to go back to school in Chicago and pay more attention to math and take science classes. It's true math and science were about facts, but facts didn't worry her as much as they used to, and they didn't seem boring. A lot of facts were as beautiful as poetry—paramecia dancing in a ballroom of water. Besides, Willa knew she'd need to know facts if she was going to be what she hoped to be: someone who paid attention to the natural world and got to know how it worked and tried to help living things survive on a healthy planet.

She wasn't sure what her job would be called when she finally grew up and found one. Would she study forestry or marine biology or oceanography or environmental science? Would she be a teacher or a researcher or a park ranger? Would she be one of those people who saved native plants from new housing and shopping developments and replanted them somewhere else? Would she collect bugs? Would she follow the migration of eagles? Would she be someone who went to city council meetings to ask for more funding for the parks, or someone who climbed to the top of a tall tree so the logging companies couldn't cut it down?

Would she be a scientific sleuth, an eco-detective, somebody who kept asking questions?

All Willa knew was that she wanted to work outside, at least sometimes.

Janie, Willa, and her mother had gone down to the beach, and her mother had run like a kid up to the waves and back, laughing hard. She wasn't a high-powered executive anymore, but just a woman on vacation, having a great time. She and Janie had walked a long way down the beach, with Willa trailing after, thinking her own thoughts. Janie and her mom had talked about books and traveling, and the choices that you made in life, and how one person could end up in Chicago and another in Seattle. They'd both agreed that chance played a large part in what happened to you, but you could still make choices and create change.

Chance, choice, change, Willa had thought, listening to the two women ahead of her. *Chance, choice, change.* Willa could see all those things in her own life now. She'd changed so much in just two months, and it was all because she'd spent a summer away from home. She could have changed if she'd gone to camp or San Diego, but chance had brought her to the Northwest. She'd chosen to learn new things, to become an eco-sleuth with Tabby and Phyllis, to become part of a larger family. And because of that, she'd changed.

Now, at the picnic table, surrounded by that larger family, with wrapping paper and plates of chocolate icing all around her, Willa thought, I'm coming back here.

She'd find a way to come back next summer.

After all, by then she'd be thirteen.